A CHALLENGE FROM THE AUTHORS

"The American public education system has prepared our surgeons, researchers, and scholars, and nurtured our artists, choreographers, and musicians. In its classrooms, generations of immigrants have learned a mutual tongue: the language of learning. And it remains our last, best hope . . .

Children *can* and *do* achieve their personal best in the public schools—particularly in those classrooms where parents and teachers take the time to educate themselves as well as each other.

Isn't it time we all stopped wondering whether our schools are good enough? Instead, let's apply ourselves to making them the best they can be. After all, the public schools and the potential to change them are within our reach."

HOW TO GET THE BEST PUBLIC SCHOOL EDUCATION FOR YOUR CHILD

Carol A. Ryan & Paula A. Sline
with Barbara Lagowski

ZEBRA BOOKS
KENSINGTON PUBLISHING CORP.

*To children
and to the parents and teachers
who educate them*

ZEBRA BOOKS

are published by

Kensington Publishing Corp.
475 Park Avenue South
New York, NY 10016

First Zebra Books Printing: January 1993

Printed in the United States of America

Contents

Acknowledgments

Grateful acknowledgment to our editor, Deborah Jurko-witz, for her interest in our project; to our agent, Sue Herner, for her determination to advocate for the cause of public education; to the hundreds of children who inspired the writing of this book; and to the outstanding parents and teachers who have shown commitment to a home-school partnership. A special thank-you to family and friends for their support and encouragement.

INTRODUCTION
Public School:
An Owner's Manual

Sharon and Peter are a married couple in their early thirties. Like most young people today, they have worked hard to complete their education, to establish careers, and to make a place for themselves within their community. And, like many two-career couples, they waited several years before having children. Now the happy parents of a precocious four-year-old girl, Sharon and Peter find themselves thinking about their future as a family—and wondering whether the public schools that played so positive a part in their lives will be equally positive for their child.

"Oh, Peter and I believe in the public schools, all right," declared Sharon. "We believe in the equal opportunity they stand for. And we know that without the public schools, we wouldn't have been as prepared for college—or for life. It's just that things have changed a lot in the last twenty years. Drugs seem to be out of control. The things we hear about test scores are discouraging. School kids don't just seem harder to reach, they seem *harder*." Sharon shrugged helplessly. "Sure, the public schools were great for us. But the schools have changed with the times. And not always for the better."

Like many of us, Sharon and Peter point to their public school years as a key factor in the equation that ultimately brought them success. And, like many of us, Sharon and Peter seem more comfortable with their memories of school days past than they are with the prospect of enrolling their daughter in the near future. They are hardly alone in their concern. Parents who are politically committed to the idea of public schools wonder whether to take the privatization of America personally and enroll their children in private schools. The single parent who prefers that her child be educated with the neighborhood kids may find herself enrolling her child in a school across town so she can take advantage of school-sponsored day care. Linguistically diverse families struggle daily to understand whether their son's bilingual program is smoothing his entry into American culture or delaying it. And we are all wondering why our elementary schools just don't seem as innocent or as kind as they were when we were young.

Or were they? A generation ago, we didn't know whether our schools were good or bad. We didn't wonder whether our teachers felt "burned out." Oh sure, there were a few "problem kids" in class, but they were no threat to us. The curriculum, perhaps, could have been more demanding, but the world wasn't as competitive then as it is now. And maybe not all of our schools were *completely* integrated.

Although our schools may not have been perfect, they were ours. From the scratchy filmstrips in the audiovisual center to the nubs of chalk beside the blackboard, there was no doubt in our minds that the school and everything in it were put there for our use.

And our parents felt just as comfortable. In fact, they began to treat the schools as they would a reliable car. Come Monday morning, they simply plunked the kids in their seats and expected the school system to run. And it *did* run, for a while. Until somewhere along the way, things began to change.

Suddenly, our schools weren't so innocent anymore. They were places with high drop-out rates and low test scores. In our inner-city schools, dedicated young educators were nearly extinct, and everywhere a disease called drug abuse spread like an epidemic. While parents blamed the teachers and teachers blamed the system, our trust in public education began to waver. Suddenly, it didn't seem as though we owned the schools, anymore. Worse, nobody seemed to know how to go about reclaiming them—until now.

WHAT THE NEWSPAPER HAVEN'T TOLD YOU

The media have done a good job informing us about what's wrong with our schools. Most parents, in fact, can recite the litany of problems as if it were a disgruntled taxpayer's credo. But what we haven't been so thoroughly informed about is what innovative researchers, school administrators, and our most progressive educators point to as the solution for these ills. From Maine to the coast of California, from America's heartland to the heart of the South, a nation of experts agrees: public education works best when parents work with it. But how can parents become true partners in a child's education? What can they do to improve teacher-student relations, test scores, and the curriculum? How can they reclaim the schools to which they have a right—and a responsibility?

AN INTRODUCTION—AND AN INVITATION

We are among the educators who will benefit from your increased involvement in the public schools. For many years we were classroom teachers on the "front lines" of public education. We are currently working daily in public elementary schools outside Boston: Paula Sline as an elementary school principal, and Carol Ryan, a school psychologist. Together we developed PROJECT "PIK-UPS" (Positive Integration of Kids in Urban and suburban Public Schools), a program designed to help students increase their self-esteem and motivation for learning. Another of our programs, the PIE PROJECT (Partnership of Industry and Education), matched the needs of public schools with the resources of industry to increase student achievement. In addition to our in-school responsibilities, we are currently education consultants who work daily to bridge the gap between students, teachers, school administrators, and *parents*, all of whom must work together if our public schools are to improve.

How can parents help our schools to be all they can be? In this book, we draw on our experiences as practitioners to fill the informational void. Yes, our elementary schools have changed since today's parents were students. And, because they reflect our constantly evolving society, they will continue to change daily. By painting a picture of the typical school day, we hope to put parents in touch with the true face of public school. Be it urban or suburban, materially or culturally enriched,

12

the beauty of your school lies in its function not as an institution but as a place where life in all its richness and diversity is explored to the fullest. It is a place where parents, too, are invited to explore life, as volunteers, aides, guest speakers, storytellers, creative artists, and even teachers.

We believe that anyone who has ever enjoyed learning is a potential educator. And anyone who has ever been a child is a potential child advocate. In this book, we hope to unlock the potential child advocate in every parent by revealing prolonged pressure to excel can thwart the enjoyment of learning. Here parents will learn the truth about test scores and the dangers of accelerated early-learning programs. Here, too, they will learn how their choice among elementary schools will shape the way their children feel about learning. And they will learn how to choose a quality school, not by its test scores, its college acceptance rates, or even its address, but by its ability to instruct and enrich the whole child.

Finally, we explore the many important ways a child's home life affects not only his grades but his hunger for learning. As parents, family members, and ex-students ourselves, we understand that many parents were educated at a time when school and home were considered totally separate realms—a time when "parental involvement" meant whipping up an extra dozen chocolate chip cookies for the class bake sale. For them, in particular, we have tried to throw open the schoolroom doors by providing step-by-step guidelines for an effective parent-teacher conference; strategies for de-stressing the homework hour; at-home techniques for bringing out the best in the special needs or gifted and talented child; and even awareness exercises to keep parents from passing down their school phobias to their children.

More than anything else, we hope to reassure all parents that a good education is *not* synonymous with a private school education. The American public education system has prepared our surgeons, researchers, and scholars, and nurtured our artists, choreographers, and musicians. In its classrooms, generations of immigrants have learned a mutual tongue: the language of learning. And it remains our last, best hope: as a living, multicultural experiment where over 24 million children annually experience the rewards of cultural diversity; as a changing, growing microcosm of our changing, growing communities; as the only institution that educates its most scathing critics as well as its vehement supporters.

Children *can* and *do* achieve their personal best in the public schools—particularly in those classrooms where parents and teachers take the time to educate themselves as well as each other.

Isn't it time we all stopped wondering whether our schools are good enough? Instead, let's apply ourselves to making them the best they can be. After all, the public schools and the potential to change them are within our reach.

I
Some Good Reasons for Going Public

In the small city where she lives, Susan is known as a real doer. She is the part-owner of her own travel agency and has researched and written a series of travel booklets. Susan is also a divorced mother of two who has recently taken on a weekend job to help to finance her sons' way through a non-sectarian private school.

"The public elementary school is right down the street," Susan said. "I'd love to be able to send Nicholas and Zachary there. But if I've learned anything since my divorce, it's that the best things in life really *aren't* free. Why should it be any different when it comes to schools?"

It isn't hard to understand why parents opt out of the public school system—even for lifelong educators, like us. The newspapers carry all the gloom and doom on public education that's fit to print—and some that isn't. By 9:00 A.M., the average parents have had their minimum daily requirement of bad news on the education front. They go off to work worried about the possibility that they have enrolled their child in an unsafe, unproductive environment. And they come home dreading that the violence, drugs, and poor test scores that plague "those other schools" in "those other towns" have hit home at last.

At its worst, the public school system creates its own critics and dissipates its supporters. But even in those school systems where public education is at its best, parents—including those who attended public schools themselves—now view it warily. Does anything positive happen in our schools? Why do bad schools get so much press? Could Susan be right? Is a free education an education without value?

HOW TO GET WHAT YOU PAY FOR

Susan is right about one thing: the best things in life are *not* free, and that includes our public schools. Much to their consternation, a "free" education is something taxpayers pay for dearly. And they have been generous. The average per-pupil expenditure for a public school student in the United States is $4,890. In several states (New York and New Jersey) spending per pupil has topped the $8,000 mark.

But are we as taxpayers getting what we pay for? We believe so. Our public elementary schools are educating over 24 million students each year. And publicly educated children are learning more than reading and math. They are learning to live in a diverse population, and to live by the values that are embraced by the world's most inclusive culture. Most of all, they are learning to value

16

themselves as the individuals who will, one day, shape that culture.

On a strictly mercenary level, well-run public schools mean higher property values which is good news for senior citizens and taxpayers with no children. Still, there is only one way to get what you pay for when it comes to public education: make your schools the best they can be.

By reading this book, you will learn what it takes to make a school work—and what you can do to make yours work better. You will come to understand that your role in your child's education only begins—not ends—when you join the Parent-Teachers Organization (or your school's PTA or Parents Advisory Council). Most of all, we hope that you will discover many, many good reasons for making public education your personal choice.

PUBLIC SCHOOLS HIT KIDS WHERE THEY LIVE

Even kids who attend private schools live in public neighborhoods. Taking them out of the community mainstream to be educated alters their perception of the world they live in and sends a negative message about the people in it.

Ethnic diversity is a strength, not a weakness. And children who take advantage of the public schools' open-door policy share in that strength. From kindergarten on, they are mainstreamed into the real world, where real people must work together to solve real problems—even if they don't speak the same language.

Unfortunately, public schools tend to reflect both the negative and positive characteristics of the environment that surrounds them. This means that they are not immune to the drugs, crime, and violence currently infecting our cities and towns. But those same schools also form the first line of defense against social concerns, often by developing their own innovative programs to deal with such cultural ills as drug abuse, high drop-out rates, and health issues.

Even if it meant taking a second job, many of us could scrimp and save enough to send our children to parochial or private school. But public school doesn't just educate its students to function within the school. It educates them for *life*. And that's something no amount of money can buy.

PUBLIC SCHOOLS PROTECT CHILDREN'S RIGHTS

There are schools that infuse their teaching with a cultural emphasis, such as Afrocentrism or the education of young women. There are parochial schools to instruct students in specific religious beliefs. But the only schools formed specifically to define and protect the educational and human rights of its students are those schools within the American public education system.

Our public schools give voice to those who have no vote—and therefore are not heard. By law, the public schools must

- *Accept children regardless of race, color, creed, sexual orientation, and socioeconomic status*. Though private schools may not discriminate overtly, it's no secret that many of them maintain an ethnic "balance" through stringent entrance testing, high academic requirements, and exorbitant tuitions.

- *Satisfy curriculum guidelines as set forth by the state department of education*. This guarantees that all children will be grounded in the educational basics and get their fair share of such boosters as art, music, and computer science.

18

- *Provide free transportation for students who live a specified distance from school.* These distance cut-offs are generally based on a local norm, but most average between one and one and a half miles. Allowances can be made when schools are located in high-risk areas or if very young children are being bused.

- *Adhere to building safety codes in order to remain open.* Some fire codes for public buildings must be met, no matter what. But some safety codes apply to private schools only if they get funding from the government.

  As a visitor, you may find that your public schools are much more "user friendly" in general, simply because of the diversity of their students. Public Law 94–142 stipulates that physically challenged kids must have everything they need—ramps, special facilities, and the like—to function independently within the school setting. It is adaptations like these that make the right to education a reality for all children.

- *Allow due process to students who are being disciplined, especially before a suspension.* This saves a child from undeserved discipline—and from becoming a target for a particular teacher's or administrator's wrath.

- *Participate in a federally subsidized lunch program for students or offer free or reduced-price lunches to those whose families qualify.* It is one thing to tell children that education can free them from the effect of poverty. This program enables us to prove it.

- *Provide special education services to all children with special needs between the ages of three and twenty-one.* Learning difficulties are truly nondiscriminatory. They span all cultures, touch all socioeconomic groups, and affect up to 20 percent of all schoolchildren (many of whom are of average to above-average intelligence). Left unchecked, learning difficulties can make mastering the three *Rs* a nearly insurmountable challenge.

Thanks to Public Law 94–142, learning doesn't have to be quite so difficult for these kids anymore. Designed to prevent frustration (and increasing drop-out rates) among students, this law provides free developmental screening for young students entering school—and help for those predisposed to learning difficulties by viruses or accidents they may have suffered in utero.

- *Provide transitional bilingual education services to linguistically diverse students who are not yet proficient in English*. This grants all children the right to learn the basics in the language in which they are most comfortable.

- *Require all children to be vaccinated before entering school*.

A PARENT'S BILL OF RIGHTS

Kids aren't the only ones whose rights are protected under the guidelines for quality public education. As a parent, you have some rights when it comes to public education, too—including the right to know some very basic bits of information about what sort of experience you can expect the public school system to provide.

For instance, you have a right to know

- *Which special programs are offered in your child's school*. That pricey private *école* may begin French instruction on the first day of kindergarten, but does it offer a readiness program for *les étudiants* who find reading—*en Anglaise*—a challenge? Are those children who require speech training segregated from the rest of the class? Is there an on-staff speech therapist?

The purpose of the public education system is to provide educational opportunity for all children, regardless of financial status or special need. The moment you enroll your child in a public school, he is eligible *by law* for any number of learning enhancement and special education programs, including transitional, gifted and talented, bilingual ed, remedial services, computer labs, speech services, counseling, music, art, physical education—and any combination of programs necessary to satisfy the needs of your child.

• *The credentials of the administrative and teaching staff in your child's school.* Public school teachers must be certified to teach in specific subject areas by the state where they work. In contrast, private school teachers need not be certified at all. Some of the time they need only satisfy the academic requirements of the administrator or headmaster to be hired.

• *School schedules, including parent conference dates and inservice days for teachers.* Some private schools may be steeped in tradition, but many of them operate the way they did fifty years ago! This is the age of the two-career family. Today's parents need to plan ahead—and the public schools, which must remain in session a certain number of hours each day and a predetermined number of days each year—enable them to do so.

• *The school's discipline code.* Private schools are not required to provide parents with a comprehensive discipline code. How can a parent prepare her child to meet the school code of conduct when it is subject to an administrator's moods and whims?

The principal at your child's public school should provide you (upon request) with a clearly drawn code of conduct, delineating detention and suspension procedures, and including a detailed outline of rules for the classroom, lunchroom, playground, and transportation system.

- *The grading standards at each grade level, including the format of the report card.* How do ungraded assignments show up in your child's report card grades? Is the teacher's assessment of completely subjective skills such as "class participation" likely to work for or against your child?

  Although no grading system is totally objective, your child's teacher should be able to explain, to your satisfaction, her scoring procedures and the way they translate to report card grades.

- *What classroom enrichment opportunities are available for average, gifted, and challenged learners.*

- *What your school's promotion and retention policies are.* Neither promotion nor retention should come as a surprise in any public school, nor should the teacher's grounds for making that judgment. As a parent, you have a right to know precisely what it will take for your child to pass from one grade to the next—and which criteria will keep him back.

- *The attendance and truancy laws in your district.* Those of us who value education think of truancy as a thing of the past. It may shock you to learn, then, that we personally have handled the cases of elementary school-age children who were absent more than 90 percent of the school year.

  There are many reasons for truancy. In homes where poverty has settled in, an elder child may be pressed into service as a baby-sitter. In other cases, an exceptionally bright child may hit the streets instead of the books if he feels unchallenged in the school setting.

But whatever the reason, too many unexcused absences could lead to Department of Social Services' intervention and/or possible retention of the student. In cases where the root cause of the problem is never addressed, it can even predispose a child to ultimately drop out of school altogether.

- *Your child's skill-level designation and how that level was determined.* It may be flattering to have your child designated as "talented." It may be disturbing to think that your greatest gift—your child—is considered "slow" by his teachers. But it is always reassuring to know that in your public school, you can find out how those designations were made—and who made them.

- *How you can become a partner in your child's education.* Children have the right to a teacher who will guide them as they dig into the work of learning—and to a principal who will encourage them to share in the rewards as well.

Some private schools actively discourage parents from taking part in the learning process, and some parents even prefer it that way. But most of today's parents are more involved in their children's daily lives than ever. For them, it is imperative to make home and school work together—and to separate the facts about public school from the fiction.

A PRIVATE CONCERN

"Of course, private school kids are more disciplined," one father snapped. "If kids don't behave in private school, they get thrown out. You can't do that in public school."

23

"I have nothing against the schools in my town. In fact, as public schools go, they're outstanding," said Roberta, a mother who had just enrolled her second son in parochial school. "I just think private school gives kids a leg up."

We have already discussed some effects of the privatization of America. And we have seen how, for some parents, buying into a private school means buying into a more rarified social milieu—even for those parents who themselves were the beneficiaries of quality public education. To most of us, that viewpoint seems more than a little myopic. Still, there is something about the mystique of private education that gives each of us pause. Have we come to believe that choosing an education is like buying an automobile, which is to say, you get what you pay for? Are we really buying into private education? Or is there something we're trying to buy our way out of?

THE THINGS THAT MONEY CAN'T BUY

"This town seems like a sleepy little resort community, but there's a major drug bust here every week," one father lamented. "Three of the houses on my street have been burglarized in the last year and a half. And the street crime has gotten so bad, you have to warn your kids about it when they leave for school. Why should I expose my kid to more of the same? Learning is hard enough as it is."

Oh, don't we all wish that a problem-free society were something that money could buy! But does this father really mean for us to believe that there are no drugs in the private school to which he has chosen to send his son? That problems we don't see are problems we don't have?

A designer education may be something we wrap ourselves in like designer jeans, but both offer just about as much protection from the ills that plague our communities. Private school is not a panacea. And public school isn't always the school of hard knocks. That is why we owe it to our children to be very sure about our reasons for choosing the schools they will attend.

CHECKLIST FOR SELECTING A SCHOOL

We all want what's best for our children. On that much, all parents can agree. But when it comes to defining a set of specific characteristics that communicate to us a high-quality, well-rounded education, those characteristics can vary widely.

Are the decisions you are making about your child's education totally free from prejudice? Would you feel differently about Lincoln Elementary if it were called Foxcroft Country Day School?

The following checklist can help you to prioritize those qualities you feel are important in a school—and to ascertain what is important to you as a parent. Simply rate the following school characteristics from one to ten, one being of greatest importance to you; ten the least.

_____ DISCIPLINE

_____ EXPERIENCE AND EDUCATION LEVEL OF STAFF

_____ HIGH STANDARDIZED TEST SCORES

_____ RELIGIOUS INSTRUCTION

_____ SAME SCHOOL THAT COLLEAGUES' CHILDREN ATTEND

_____ LOCATION/CONDITION OF SCHOOL

_____ HEALTH, DRUG, SEX EDUCATION PROGRAMS

_____ PARENT INVOLVEMENT

_____ INDIVIDUALIZED INSTRUCTION/SPECIAL ED

_____ ETHNIC/CULTURAL MIX OF STUDENTS

Now take a look at what makes up your top five.

If *discipline* is most important to you, it may be time to think hard about what constitutes an acceptable discipline policy in your mind. Is it corporal punishment? Some private schools rely on the paddle, which they call "the board of education." Is it the mere appearance of discipline? There is nothing that looks more orderly—even if it is not—than a class dressed in matching uniforms.

Certainly order needs to be maintained in the classroom. But one does not develop a creative, disciplined mind through the constant correction of a child's behavior. In fact, too much correction can stifle the imagination altogether and even lead to a feeling of insecurity.

If the *experience and education level of staff* ranks high on your list, your mind is in the right place for seeking out the best education for your child. But are you looking in the right place? Only public schools require their teachers to be certified to teach by the state in which they work. And only public schools demand that teachers be certified in those subjects they will teach.

What about private schools? In a private school with a private charter, only the headmaster or principal must be certified. All other personnel are excused from meeting state regulations (much to the surprise of some parents).

If *high standardized test scores* seem like a nice, verifiable yardstick with which to quantify a quality education, you should know that test scores can and do come up short. They may even be a sign of some creative test taking on the part of the school administrators. (For more complete information on the merits and fallacies of standardized testing, see chapter 3.)

Religious instruction is an indisputable reason for sending a child to private or parochial school—as long as religious instruction is not offered instead of equally important academic pursuits. Be sure that the education your

26

child receives is well-rounded. Ask the administrators of both the private and public schools which subjects are taught each day and how much time is spent on each subject. It will give you a basis for comparison.

If *having your children attend the same school that your colleagues' children attend* made the top of your list, you get top marks for honesty. It's one thing to make a decision about our children's education that we are comfortable with. But defending that decision to "well-meaning" colleagues, friends, and especially relatives is quite another.

Take a lesson from the common-sense play book: the best defense is still a great offense. Know your school and the reasons you chose it, and no one can ever shake you from your position.

You can't tell a book by its cover—and you can't tell anything about a school by its *location or condition*, either. Sure, the local parochial school may be situated on the very best parcel of parish land, but does it offer the *health, drug, sex education programs* you feel are so important? That charming private school may have gothic arches, but how often are parents encouraged to pass under them? Is *parental involvement* encouraged? Is it even tolerated?

And what about *individualized instruction or special ed* programs that may benefit your child? Many private schools simply find it too costly to keep specialists like speech therapists, special education teachers, or even guidance counselors on staff. In those cases, your child may find himself having to receive the services of a specialist at the local public school, or going without.

If the *ethnic mix* of students did not show up in your top five, perhaps now is the time for you to reconsider.

A school whose population does not reflect the cultural diversity of the community outside it is a school that cannot prepare its students for life in the real world. We cannot state our case more clearly than that. As it now stands, American citizens know less about what goes on in the rest of the world than any other developed nation. Few of us know any language besides English. Most of us know nothing of world geography, nor do we have any clear idea about how cultural differences influence the way human beings think. Yet, armed with an understanding of our neighbors that is skin deep, we set out to live together as "equals."

Do we really wish to pass on that kind of cultural illiteracy to our children?

Finally, when you visit any private school, look beyond its architecture, its reputation, and its prestige. That's when you will see its true face. Then take a second look at your public school. There is probably no more accurate reflection of your diverse community—or of your personal values.

2
Bureaucracy 101:
A Crash Course
for Parents

I don't know. It's not my department.
—SCHOOL BOARD SECRETARY'S RESPONSE WHEN
ASKED THE DATE SCHOOL SYSTEM REPORT
CARDS WOULD BE ISSUED IN THE STATE OF
NEW JERSEY

As we said before, the beauty of public education lies in its ability to teach to and learn from its students in all of their diversity. There are over 24 million students currently enrolled in 70,000 public schools across the United States, each of them with a unique set of needs, challenges, and talents. Reaching them is a big job, with big costs, requiring a support staff of thousands.

Bureaucracy may not be a four-letter word, but we have a feeling that the educational bureaucracy may have inspired a few. Defined as a "body of officials and administrators," the *B* word has become synonymous with inefficiency. It is the tag line of the creative quagmire, the hallmark of the lumbering colossus. To many of the citizens who support it through their state and local taxes, the educational bureaucracy is a hole in the hierarchy where taxpayers pour their money.

It's bad enough when a bureaucracy seems to be an authoritative jumble to those outside it. But it's even worse when it seems to have become a jumble in the minds of the bureaucrats themselves. Pick up the phone. Ask a member of the department of education a simple question, like who determines whether AIDS is an appropriate subject for discussion in a child's sex education class. It may not take long before you're convinced that the answer to your question is "not this office."

Still, what holds the educational bureaucracy together is not red tape but its sense of commitment. It exists solely to protect the rights of schoolchildren. It has implemented affirmative action laws and enforced length-of-day laws. It provides the basic safeguards that entitle all our children to an education, regardless of their race, socioeconomic background, or special needs.

Nor is this bureaucracy a lumbering giant that promises to be all things to all people and then serves none. The United States invests more of its resources in the education of its children than any other nation. And it will continue to educate a higher percentage of its population than any other country even as its population approaches the 300 million mark.

Don't get the idea we are letting a costly, cumbersome government bureaucracy off the hook. But the educational hierarchy is the pipeline through which all good things (like funding) flow. By turning off to it, we may be inadvertently turning off the flow of state and federal monies to our local schools.

The good news is that the educational bureaucracy need not be an impenetrable dehumanizing machine. On the local level, it can be as personable as your child's teacher and as knowledgeable as the school principal. It can even be a source of satisfaction, if you stop thinking of the bureaucracy as the barrier in front of you and start thinking of it as the structure behind you.

THE FIRST LINK IN THE CHAIN OF COMMAND

The first stop for any parent who has a question or problem relating to his child's schooling should be at the teacher's door. Of all the links in the educational chain of command, the teacher can be the strongest. Why? Simply because your child's educator has the strongest personal link to your child. Even if school has only been in session for three weeks, your child's teacher has spent those weeks getting to know each of his students. He has a handle on your child's capabilities and weaknesses and a vested interest in turning those weaknesses to strengths. Because he cannot hope to accomplish this goal without your help, he will be interested in your problems as well as your positive thoughts on what quality education should be.

The classroom teacher represents the bottom line of the public education system. It is with him that the school system has its origin and its end. In that unique position, the teacher is connected in various ways to nearly everyone who can make the difference between an outstanding learning experience and a satisfactory or a poor one, including other educators, teacher aides, administrators, secretaries, counselors, and even custodians. Moreover, the classroom teacher is a trusted colleague of the one person most directly responsible for the day-to-day running of everything that goes on in the school building, from the quality of the educational opportunity to the viability of the work environment: the school principal.

31

She looks at papers. She walks around the halls during lunch period. And she talks in the morning over the intercom.
—*A SIX-YEAR-OLD ON WHAT A PRINCIPAL DOES*

You'd better believe a principal looks at papers. A whole mess of papers! That's because the principal's function is to implement and monitor all the plans that contribute to the overall effectiveness of a school. The principal heads up the staff, functions as the bottom-line decision maker on school policy, kicks off new programs, supervises and evaluates personnel, and acts as the liaison between the school and the community that supports it. Not only does the buck often stop at the principal's office, but so do memoranda from every level of the educational bureaucracy. On any given day, the principal is likely to hear from the plant manager, a disgruntled teacher, the president of the PTO, the superintendent of schools, and the plumber who has promised to fix the toilet that was stuffed with paper towels at morning recess. No wonder school principals are known to take a walk during lunch hour. It's a wonder more of them don't walk right out the door!

To the teachers, the principal is the top dog. To the school board members and other elected officials, she is the protector of the bottom line. To the members of the PTO, the principal is the person in the middle; the twenty-four-hour mediator-on-call who smooths relations between teachers and parents, calms teacher-student disputes, irons out problems between the school staff and central office personnel, and ventures where even some American presidents will not willingly go: to the media.

People—even those people who earn their livings

within the school system—tend to view the principal's role from their own vantage point. That's easy to do. The most effective principal is a jack-of-all-trades who is willing to share her trade secrets with others. But that's what can make her such an invaluable resource to parents.

RECOGNIZING THE WELL-PRINCIPLED PRINCIPAL

If a school has high test scores and a low drop-out rate, then that school probably has a good principal. Isn't that how it works?
> —JEANNIE, AGE THIRTY-SEVEN

The only good principal is a dead principal.
> —DEAN, AGE TEN

It is easy for us to recognize those homes in which we are made to feel comfortable and welcome. Whether they are old or new, whether they are furnished in the height of fashion or with the latest hand-me-downs, there is something about them—and the people in them—that makes us feel at ease.

When you walk into a school, it is nearly like walking into a home the principal has built. The people you see there—from the secretaries in the office to the teachers and the students—are part of the school community. What they are doing in that building is creating an environment for learning. If you, as a visitor or a volunteer, are received in a way that makes you feel welcome, you can bet that you have found a principal who will make your children feel at home with education.

Of course, we can hear the principals laughing as we write this. If a school feels like a principal's home, it's because she spends so much time there! True enough. But a parent doesn't have to spend too much time there to get a "feel" for a school. Test scores can be misleading; they may be under par even if a principal is topnotch. But taking note of a school's atmosphere will never leave you with the wrong impression.

Is the principal accessible? She is if you feel more like a welcomed guest than a pesky salesperson. The principal can be a parent's powerful ally—but a wise principal will see you as a valued ally as well. She will tackle your problems headon and answer your questions honestly. Many principals even keep their doors open most of the time and, when they are not available, have a mailbox or other mechanism in use so that parents, staff, and students can always keep in touch. Some maintain suggestion boxes in a quiet corner where parents drop off their comments without dropping in on the principal herself.

Of course, there must be limits to such an open-door policy. Parents cannot be allowed to tamper with the education process. Nor should they expect the principal to be at their beck and call. Still, an open, creative attitude is a good sign—especially if it is allowed to flow down through the entire chain of command.

And that includes the students as well as the teachers. Does the principal seem to know most students by name? That is the mark of a caring educator. Does she maintain an easy, collegial give-and-take with the teachers? Do the teachers share their secret techniques and areas of expertise with one another? That is the sign of an administrator who is doing her best to bring out the best in her staff.

Contrary to Dean's opinion, a principal should be very much alive—and so should the school. Take a walk down the hall, and make note of what you see. Is there a culture at work in the school? Do the school bulletin boards reflect the vitality of its students? Are projects on display? Are there posters advertising an upcoming event like a food drive, car wash, or bake sale? A creative school run by a vital administrator feels alive and energetic—not closed, quiet, or paranoid.

This is not to say that the principal should be so amenable and approachable that he becomes what your kids would call "a wuss." Public schools are protected by law in terms of what they must offer, so there is uniformity, to a great extent, from school to school within a city. But there is definitely *not* uniformity in extra projects that need funding, repairs required on a particular school, or the additional teacher who might make a qualitative difference in a child's life. If the school principal lacks the courage to fight for her school, to fire ineffective personnel, or confront the controversial issues, chances are her school will lag behind others in creativity and effectiveness. The principal may wear many hats, but she should always carry the banner of child advocacy. If yours seems hesitant to "bother" the superintendent or if she spends more time at meetings and conferences than in the school, your child may not be getting the representation he needs to get the most out of public education.

We aren't recommending that you go to the school to spy, but we do suggest that you go to the school to learn. If you have a question about school policy, a concern about your child or your child's teacher, ask the principal. It is her job to serve as a liaison between home and school.

Remember: the principal who does not make herself accessible to you may not be any more accessible to those officials who make the budgetary decisions for your district. Because of the principal's attitude, then, your child may get the short end of the pointer. But a principal who is enthusiastic and energetic, who gives generously of her assistance, feedback, and support can be a boon to her students, a much-needed backup for harried parents, and an inspiration to her staff.

The most you can do for her is to return the favor—by providing her with the most effective superintendent and school board you possibly can.

THE SUPERINTENDENT

"I probably should be too embarrassed to admit this, but I really don't know what a superintendent of schools does," confessed John, a successful businessman and the father of two. Then he added, "By the way, who *is* the superintendent of schools, anyway? Does anybody actually know?"

In many ways, the superintendent of schools is the invisible bureaucrat. Generally speaking, his duties do not put him in the public eye. He doesn't schmooze with students or even parents. Rather, his presence is evident in the efficiency, sensitivity, and overall philosophy (or lack of it) by which the school system is run.

Whether all bureaucrats should be invisible (or at least inaudible) is an arguable point. What is not debatable, however, is the importance of a knowledgeable superintendent. He is the person who works directly with the school principals in his district, who holds regular meetings with administrators, evaluates their performance, arranges for staffing in each school, and acts as the conduit between the school principals and the rest of the educational scheme.

These duties alone constitute a big job. Just evaluating school principals is a time-consuming proposition, requiring the superintendent to spend hours in each school (and away from his desk) in order to see its principal in action. But hiring and firing at high levels isn't the only concern of the superintendent. Nor is it the only way that what the superintendent does (and how well he does it) affects the entire community.

The superintendent of schools is the bridge between the community and the state and federal departments of education. As such, it is his job to see to it that the schools within his district get their share of the economic pie. In these days of hiring freezes, education cutbacks, and in some states, outright tax revolts, each slice of pie can amount to little more than a starvation ration. But the battles for each additional penny of funding are waged to the death.

That's why the superintendency has become an express ticket to professional burnout, especially for superintendents who must contend with larger systems—and larger problems. Although in many districts there is an assistant superintendent (and often several associates under him) to help with day-to-day operations, the superintendent is scheduled to the max. Between his regular office hours and evening meetings, from the first crisis of the morning to twelfth-hour contract negotiations, he is always on the run. That can leave little time for running the school system, and little energy for dealing with the most powerful local body of all: the school board.

THE MEMBERS OF THE BOARD

"There's Helen—her special interest is funding high school athletics. You know her boy . . . he's first string center on the basketball team this year. Then, of course, there's Fred. He's a fixture. And next to him, that's Bobby—quit school at sixteen. Now he's running the schools. Yup—that's our school board. And if more people knew it, they'd stop wondering why the schools are such a mess.''

All school boards are not created equal. Nor are they all created in the image and likeness of the one described above. But they *are* political bodies. And they are made up of locally elected officials. That makes the school board subject to local prejudices and preferences. In the worst possible cases, school board decisions are made solely on the basis of personal prejudice, making the board an ideal forum for the individual ego—but a lousy place to air issues of public concern. In those towns, school board elections run like a broken revolving door. Nobody new can get in. The incumbents can't be gotten out. And year after year, the same old people just keep on going around and around.

It is so easy to tell when a school board is in trouble that even children can do it. And they often do. If your fifth grader comes home complaining that there are not enough cassette tape players in the language lab but the hockey team has new ''away'' uniforms, it's time for you to race down to the next school board meeting. Once there, you only have to listen and learn. If the public is not encouraged to speak, if no board member wants to take responsibility for the budget, if there are no set criteria for school board membership (like a high school education), or if individual board members seem more like calcified fixtures than enthusiastic participants, your town has school board problems. And those are the kind of problems no community can afford.

The money that pays for your schools comes from a number of sources, including local taxes, state revenues, and federal funds. The people who determine how that money will be spent are the local men and women you elect to the school committee. Often school officials don't know how much money they can expect to receive from state and federal sources until July or August. That simple fact of fiscal life may make long-range financial planning impossible on the local level, but it might also make the school committee a more vital, spontaneous body. On a day-to-day basis, your school board grapples with such issues as whether a new school needs to be built, whether old schools are being properly maintained, whether the school budget should equal that of other municipal departments, and whether an old text (or an old superintendent) needs to be retired. These are the decisions that can make a difference in a child's daily life. And unless you are present and accounted for at the next school board meeting, they will be made without you.

The point of public school is to offer a broad spectrum of experiences to a broad spectrum of students. Therefore, the ideal school board is an amalgam of every type of citizen that makes up the community. Helen, whose son has made the varsity basketball team, may be a great asset to the school board—once her opinion is balanced by members who happen to be parents of middle-school and elementary-level students. Taxpayers who have no kids in school may ensure that the school board is more than a convenient place to grind a favorite ax. Experienced citizens or retired business people can bring a sense of fiscal responsibility to the business of education. And minority members will ensure that ethnically diverse students are represented, both in the hiring of qualified minority teachers and in the implementation of programs that may be of special interest to minority students.

But the job of the school board is not to administrate the schools. That is the principal's milieu. The merits and demerits of a particular teacher's personality should not be a school board concern. Those should be brought up with the principal—or, in extreme cases, the superintendent. Most of all, the school board should refrain from dabbling in those decisions that belong to those who truly direct it, those who make up the very hierarchy that drives them to distraction: the real bureaucrats—us.

CUTTING THE RED TAPE

"I've always been a space buff," said Tony, the father of a son who inherited his father's hobby as well as his name. "So when I looked through Tony Jr.'s science book, I nearly flipped. It was so out of date, it didn't even include space-age technology!

"I assumed the teacher would be as surprised by it as I was, but she just sent me to the principal. The principal looked at the book and then referred me to the school committee. I cornered the head of the school board at the next meeting. At that point, I thought for sure I'd get some action, but all he did was say that he'd have to check on it. You see, it might not matter whether rocket boosters are covered in the science text. Not if space-age technology isn't considered third-grade curriculum."

Tony shook his head. "I know it's human nature for these people to protect their jobs, but my kid has to be educated! Where does the buck stop?"

Often, what seems to be a simple question to a parent like Tony cannot be answered without calling on several different levels of the educational bureaucracy.

Matters of curriculum—like the inclusion of space-age technology in a third-grade text—pose just such difficulties. The scope of a school's curriculum—what it will and will not teach—is shaped jointly by state and local authorities. These decisions are also influenced by other factors, such as the range of knowledge required by standardized tests and state assessment guidelines. (The truth

40

is that, to one degree or another, nearly all school districts "teach to the tests.") But the materials used to teach each subject, books, audio tapes, films, et cetera, are selected locally, usually by the school committee.

In the best of all possible worlds, the school board would have owned up to its responsibility for out-of-date books. Perhaps the principal might have asked that a curriculum review committee be formed to identify any other outmoded teaching materials. Many school districts have already begun restructuring in order to make their administrators and educators more accountable to the parents and students they serve.

But while that restructuring is taking place, your children are in school. What can a parent like Tony do to get answers at the local level? The purpose of the educational system is to empower all its citizens. So why does it make us feel so powerless?

The bureaucracy in any organization is the sum of all its members. The best way to beat the educational bureaucracy, then, is to join it! Here's what you can do:

- *Give your child a voice at election time.* Even in those towns where education is a political hot potato, voter turnout can be dismal when the school board members are up for election. Of course, it is important that you make yourself heard in state and federal level races. But your local officials are the ones with one hand on the schools and the other on your wallet!

  Whether you vote a candidate in, vote a candidate out, or neglect to cast a vote at all, you are sending your elected officials a message about your concern— or your apathy. Don't go by the slogans when seeking out the candidate who has your child's best interests in mind. Actions speak louder than words in the political arena. Check the candidate's voting record on educational issues—then double-check any discrepancy between what he *says* he'll do and what he has done.

The same advice applies when voting at the state or federal level, but there is one additional thing to keep in mind: you don't just vote for a governor or president; you vote for that candidate's appointees as well. In other words, one of the politicos dancing at the inaugural ball tonight may be deciding the fate of your school system tomorrow. Read the papers. Be aware. It's the only way of knowing whom you're really voting for.

• *Make your child's voice heard locally.* You are already investing a huge percentage of your local taxes in your child's education. Isn't it worth a few hours of your time to protect that investment?

You may be harried. You may be hassled. But there isn't a parent on earth who can't pay at least two visits a year to the local school board meeting. Why two? Once to find out what the school committee is up to—and again to do something about it!

In most communities, there are two meetings a year that parents would find particularly interesting: the budget meeting, during which expenditures are discussed and voted upon, and the goal-setting meeting, at which the philosophy of the school system is set forth. Check the newspapers to see what's on the school board agenda. Or ask the school principal which meetings she feels you should attend. An upcoming session may be of particular interest to you and your child.

Then do yourself and your school system a favor: bring along a friend who may not have school-age children or whose children attend a local private school. Their taxes (like yours) keep the educational system running smoothly. By getting them involved in how that money is spent, they are encouraged to buy into the system—and to improve it, whether they have children who use it or not.

- *Stand by your principals*. The school principal is your first line of defense against an impersonal bureaucracy, and the first stepping stone to a better one. Make certain she is given the power and the authority she needs to lead—and the salary she needs to live.

  If the position of principal in your school seems to be regarded as a temporary one, find out why. It takes time for an administrator to get to know her school, to shake up those departments that need changing, and to shore up those that are functioning well. Positive results can't be sustained if your town is constantly putting out the "help wanted" sign.

- *Let the buck stop with you*. An unimaginative, complacent bureaucracy can only flourish where there are unimaginative, complacent parents.

  Educational excellence isn't something you find— it's something you build. Roll up your sleeves. The bureaucracy will work for you when you begin to work with it.

schools had similar budgets. And by law, both schools

3
In Search of Educational Excellence

Dara and Terrence—the parents of two school-age daughters—had a lot to be proud of. Dara had been out of the work force for five years, but as soon as Keeshia, her younger child, was ready for school, Dara found a job as a publicist at the community theater. Terrence was a counselor in a drug intervention program. He, Dara, Keeshia, and Kyla spent their weekends renovating the older home they had purchased in a small, ethnically mixed city—until they ran into a situation that wasn't so easily remedied. The family's new home was in a district where there were two elementary schools. It was up to them to decide which their children would attend.

There were many similarities between the Howland Avenue School and John Adams Elementary. Both included grades one through six. Their student bodies were of similar size and ethnic makeup; they were taught by a roughly equivalent number of teachers and aides. Both schools had similar budgets. And by law, both schools could be expected to provide the family with special services, an item of interest since Keeshia had a number of speech problems. It seemed as though the decision would be an academic toss-up, until Dara made an appointment to visit the Howland Avenue School.

How far will parents go to ensure that their children are receiving the utmost in enrichment and education? Some couples we know travel miles each day to deliver their offspring to the doors of a "wealthier" school system. Others have uprooted entire families, as if trucking them to a different town or state would provide their children with a more compelling "view" of the educational landscape.

We all want to feel that we have afforded our children the best that public education has to offer. That's the stuff the American dream is made of. But how do we go about finding the school system of our dreams? What characteristics make up the "ideal" school? A limitless budget? Innovative programs? High test scores? How do parents' perceptions of quality education differ from those of teachers and administrators? Would we even recognize a quality school if we found one?

At first glance, Howland Avenue seemed like the last place Dara wanted to send her children. The building was well maintained but old. And the same description could have applied to the principal. She seemed kindly and caring. She even greeted the children by name as she escorted Dara to her office. But she was hardly the type to introduce any earth-shattering new programs—or at least, that was what Dara had heard from one of her new neighbors, the mother of a dyslexic child.

But it wasn't long before Dara found herself doubting the neighborhood scuttlebutt. The principal wasn't old— she was *experienced*. And it was apparent that she enjoyed a good, collegial relationship with the teachers, all of whom chatted briefly as they passed to their classrooms.

What's more, the principal had made a great effort to keep Howland Avenue up-to-date. Because she felt strongly about mainstreaming children with special needs, the principal would make it possible for Keeshia to work with a speech therapist inside the standard classroom. What's more, Howland Avenue School had recently introduced school-based after-school care. Dara and Terrence would not have to seek out a reliable sitter among a city of strangers. Kyla and Keeshia could remain at school—under the watchful eye of a certified teacher— until their parents picked them up!

On her way out, Dara took a last look at Howland Avenue School. Funny, but the building didn't look so old to her anymore. It looked hopeful and welcoming.

Dara had gone to check out an old school and found a new opportunity. She couldn't wait to tell Terrence— and the kids—the great news.

ALL PUBLIC SCHOOLS ARE NOT CREATED EQUAL

This nation is founded on the democratic principle of equal opportunity for all—and so are our schools. But that doesn't mean that all public schools are created equal.

Magnet schools are thematic schools, often located in our inner cities, that have been reenergized with state or federal dollars and restructured to specialize in certain areas of study (for instance, the arts, theater and drama, computer skills, mathematics, or science). Many of them have distinguished themselves nationwide, functioning as academic hothouses where our most innovative teachers and eager students can flourish. Some even have entrance requirements.

While not designated as magnet schools, many public elementary schools excel in particular fields. In some financially gifted districts, where the tax base is sufficient to support long-term student enrichment, the curriculum is more challenging across the board. Other schools—including many in financially deprived areas—strive for excellence because the educators there view achievement as crucial to the development of the whole child.

In addition, each school has its own distinct personality which may be a reflection of its leadership, staff morale, the community in which it exists, or all three. Some are more reserved, opening their doors only to students and their parents. Others are outgoing, offering a range of programs and community outreach services that touch many sectors of the community. Ironically, these "outgoing" systems are often praised in the media but penalized by concerned parents. By publicizing their solutions to community problems (such as drop-out and drug education programs which now exist at the elementary level), they inadvertently publicize the fact that the problems exist. To some parents, that means just one thing: "Hard problems—hard school."

A GOOD SCHOOL CHECKLIST

In a country where quality education is considered a basic right, why are good schools so hard to find?

In many ways, recognizing a good school is like recognizing an ideal mate: we may know one when we see one, but it isn't easy to define. Even an A-for-effort kind of school like Howland Avenue, for example, might be passed over because of its looks, or its principal's looks, or the looks of the student body.

Another reason that good schools seem hard to find is that so few of us really look! Year after year, schools open their doors to the public. And year after year, there are children enrolled in public schools whose parents have never crossed the threshold. To see a good school is to know a good school. But you'll never see one unless you take the time to visit. And when you do, be sure to take this checklist with you. It will help you separate the great schools from the merely good.

- *Is the school safe?* A child simply cannot learn in a poorly maintained environment. Leaking ceilings are, at the very least, distracting; uncovered radiators are dangerous; and peeling paint is an outright menace. As you and your child tour the school, take special note of any maintenance problems that could pose a physical hazard. And be sure to ask about any potential problems you can't see, such as asbestos fibers and radon gas. The school principal should be able to offer you proof that the school has been tested recently for both.

- *What is its personality?* The personality of a school is not like the personality of a friend. You should not discover its quirks over time. A good school should make its philosophy available—in writing—to the parents and guardians of all its students. Included in this information sheet should be methods of discipline, recommended amounts of homework for each grade, and even a brief outline of the school's goals.

  Pay special attention if your local school has been accredited—or is pursuing accreditation—by a state or regional body. Accreditation is awarded only after a school submits to examination by a visiting team of superintendents, principals, teachers, parents, or business people. An accredited school therefore, is one that has successfully put its philosophy, goals, curriculum, teacher-student ratio, and staff to the test.

Even if your local public elementary school is still pursuing accreditation, you can usually take it as a sign that the administration is serious about providing a well-rounded educational experience for your child.

- *Is it well-staffed?* Imagine yourself trying to teach a simple technique—like how to fold a paper airplane—to a group of ten second graders. In a normal classroom setting, perhaps five of those children would be eagerly and quietly folding their paper. Two others might also be folding their airplanes, but with the added challenge of having missed steps two and five. In the corner, one child not only has completed his plane, but is using it as a weapon against his neighbor. Now imagine yourself trying to teach the same technique to twenty energetic seven-year-olds. Or to thirty.

It will probably surprise you to learn that there is no data that cites teacher-student ratio as a factor critical to learning. (In our lighter moments we wonder whether it's because no teachers survived the testing!) But even if we do accept the premise that the number of students in a class has no measurable impact on standardized test scores, we merely have to imagine the scenario above to know that it has a tremendous effect on "classroom culture." And teachers agree. In a recent pool, they pin-pointed ten to fifteen student per class as the ideal teacher-student ratio; fifteen to twenty-five students per class as the ideal teacher-student ratio; fifteen to twenty-five students is preferable; twenty-five to thirty is acceptable; and more than thirty is intolerable.

In our experience, the normal primary school class includes twenty-five students, though no kindergarten class should really be larger than fifteen to eighteen kids. Keep that in mind when you ask about your child's class size. The teacher should be there to instruct—not to referee.

Be sure to ask what special credentials your child's teacher holds. Certification is a requirement, but parents are often surprised at the depth of an elementary school-teacher's knowledge. You may not think it's important to know that the music teacher is an award-winning concert pianist until your son shows an interest in the piano—or until a teacher with a special ed background recognizes that your chatterbox daughter is gifted in the language arts.

- *Is the curriculum appropriate?* Don't just stand there waiting for your child's teacher to look your way—flip through those science texts, spelling workbooks, and readers! Do they seem up-to-date? Are they likely to inspire creativity? Are they geared toward enjoyment and discovery or toward test results?

  A parent can learn a great deal about a school's philosophy by checking out what the teachers plan to teach. But don't undo the good you've done by pre-teaching the material you've seen. It will make the teacher's lesson plan old hat. And try not to "encourage" your child by hinting at good things to come. Egging a child on with teasers like, "Oh, wait till you see the story on page ten. You'll love it!" can dilute a child's sense of excitement and discovery.

- *Are its methods up-to-date?* It may not surprise you to learn that grouping—categorizing and teaching groups of children by their tested abilities—has been shown to be a less effective teaching method. Some parents may even feel that as children, *they* were grouped incorrectly and that this all-too-common error brought them an uncommon amount of pain.

  When teaching methods or theories have been shown

to be problematic, it is a school's responsibility to phase them out promptly. And it is a parent's responsibility to learn about the findings that could affect the quality of his child's education.

More research is under way right now in the field of education than ever before. Some is thorough; some is downright questionable. The school principal will be able to help you sort out which is which, and to understand whether the findings are pertinent to the schools in your community.

- *Is the school alive?* The very best schools are bursting with energy, and they put it out there for all to see. If the bulletin boards, student newspaper, or class projects on display in your local schools energize *you*, you can be sure that there is some pretty vigorous learning going on.

  But no living thing exists in a vacuum—and that goes double for schools. Festivals, ethnic celebrations, and outreach projects are all signs that a school is an active part of the community—and that the community is a vital part of it.

- *Is the principal interested in your child?* Of course, your child's teacher will express an interest. Learning—the gathering and sharing of one's thoughts—is one of the most intimate human processes of all. And for the upcoming year, you, your child, and her teacher will be partners in that process.

  The school principal is interested not only in the life of the mind but in the life of the school. It is up to her to discover what your child will bring to the school culture—and how the school culture can best benefit your child.

  The interested principal will take the time to get to know each child. She will ask what the student likes to do, what kinds of toys he prefers to play with, or whether he enjoys being read to. She may even ask if the child likes school, then bear the answer like a trooper. (Every self-respecting child knows the correct answer to that question—whether they enjoy school or not!)

In some school systems, parents are even given questionnaires about their children's preferences and personalities. These are then kept on file where they can be referred to by an interested teacher, counselor, or principal.

GETTING DOWN TO DATA

Student data, teacher credentials, and philosophical tracts aren't the only pieces of information kept on file at the local school. For some well-meaning parents, the data that matter most are so simple they can reduce a school to a single number: the standardized test score.

In the anecdote that began this chapter, Dara did many things right. She visited the school, met with the principal, toured the building. In other words, Dara took an active role in finding a nurturing, creative learning environment for her daughters.

What Terrence took, meanwhile, was the easy way out. While his wife was exploring the halls of Howland Avenue School, he did a little research himself. But instead of stopping in to see what was going on at John Adams Elementary, he drove straight past the school to the town library. He didn't want to listen to what he called "teacher talk." He wanted the facts.

When Dara came home, bubbling over with excitement about the new school year, Terrence was ready. "Look at this,'' he said, waving a photocopy of the local paper. ''John Adams Elementary not only scored higher than average on its standardized tests, it scored higher than Howland Avenue two years running!''

At first Dara argued the point. At Howland Avenue, Keeshia wouldn't have to leave her regular class to get the speech therapy she needed. Both children would be well cared for in the after-school program. Plus Dara trusted the principal. Didn't that count for something?

''Sure it does. I think it's great that we live in a town with two good schools,'' agreed Terrence. ''But maybe John Adams is just a little bit better. Besides, don't we owe it to Keeshia and Kyla to give them the edge?''

Did John Adams' students simply test better? Or were higher test scores a characteristic of a better school? Suddenly Dara wasn't so sure of her feelings anymore. But she was sure of one thing. ''Of course, I want to give the girls an edge—if there is one,'' she sighed. ''I'll visit John Adams in the morning.''

It would be a rare parent, indeed, who could make a qualitative choice between two schools without weighing their quantitative values as they are measured by standardized tests. Oh, sure, we have all heard that such tests are skewed by economic and cultural factors. They can't even be trusted to be nonsexist. But if state-of-the-art, fill-in-the-dot tests are not indicative of an individual student's achievement or a school system's success rate, why do our school systems continue to administer them? What *do* they measure? And how far do schools go to help their students measure up?

Standardized tests measure a student's performance not against his classmates but against a national standard. At their best, these tests give parents an opportunity to check that their schools' scores are progressing from year to year—and that they do not deviate too widely from state or national scores. Parents should be careful, however, not to automatically equate low scores with bad schools. Students are most likely to succeed when they are tested the way they are taught. For that reason children who are being taught developmentally or whose instruction has been individualized can fall short when tested uniformly. In some schools, below-average scores are symptomatic of a curriculum that needs revision. Discovering a curriculum deficit is bound to disturb parents and educators alike. And in those schools where curriculum has not been revised for a very long time (sometimes a decade or more) parents *should* be very concerned. But in an otherwise well-run school, the need for curriculum revision is, in itself, no cause for concern.

The educational needs of our children are organic. They are in constant flux, changing with the times or with our understanding of the times. A school administrator who makes curriculum development an ongoing process may make parents uncomfortable. The administrator may even make them feel as though their school is always playing academic "catch-up." In those schools a curriculum gap can be the result of parental reluctance—or the symptom of a stagnant school system.

Finally, standardized test scores are particularly poor indicators of quality in schools where the population is heavily bilingual. In bilingual programs, the coursework is routinely adapted to keep students challenged but not overwhelmed. Measuring those children against an instrument designed to test native English speakers is unfair to them and to their schools. In addition, standardized tests do not take into account the problems of children with nonvisual learning styles or learning difficulties.

They may be every bit as intelligent as the top scorers but rank in the lowest percentiles.

TEACHING TO THE TEST

As you have seen, there are quality schools—schools that stay within the letter of the law—that test badly. What you probably don't know is that there are also schools that believe they cannot afford the stigma of low scores. Frightened by the prospects of lost revenues and disgruntled parents, they withdraw their bilingual and special ed students from the testing. Or they change their educational goals from creating good readers to creating high test scores.

"Test-taking is a skill that I was never taught," one parent argued. "Because of my low standardized test scores, I was rejected by the graduate school I wanted to go to most. If all test scores are skewed, then why can't schools teach the test? The scores aren't considered accurate anyway, and it might give a kid a leg up."

We are not devil's advocates against high test scores—nor are we against teaching testing skills like the process of elimination and deductive reasoning. But as one educator put it, "If we had a school whose students were scoring shockingly low on a vision test, it would certainly be misguided to have classes focusing on the memorization of eye charts."

We understand why Terrence and countless other parents think twice before sending their children to a good school with low scores. No one wants to sacrifice his child to the ideal of public education. But when you choose a school solely on the basis of its test scores, you run the risk of doing precisely that. Students who test well in reading comprehension don't necessarily enjoy reading. Likewise, those who perform well on number-sequencing drills (like multiplication tables) may find themselves at a loss when playing a simple game of store. The shopkeeper may know that $2 \times 3 = 6$, but have no idea that twenty-five pennies equal one quarter.

What we're trying to say is, it is crucial for educators and parents to keep their eyes on the prize. Learning is exciting. It should be its own reward. Students who are taught how to be assessed may be prepared for the next standardized test. But those who are shown the fun of learning for learning's sake are prepared both for the test and for life.

IF SCORES ARE LOWER THAN YOU'D LIKE . . .

It is time for action, not reaction. You may consider the class performance a crime, but your child's teacher was only the witness to it. Don't put educators on the defensive by pointing the finger at them. Instead, ask about any variables in test administration that may have affected the scores.

Test results are often skewed by classroom events. A loud noise, an upsetting behavior problem, or any other interruption during the testing can disrupt the entire class's concentration. So can time of day or day of the week the test is administered make a difference of several points in the average scores. Were the students tested first thing in the morning? Or right after lunch when children are often sluggish? Was the test given on a Monday, when most kids are still in "weekend mode"? Were they surprised by it?

So much interest and angst are invested in whether our children know how to take standardized tests that we tend to overlook the issue of whether our teachers know how to administer them. To maximize scores, children should be made as comfortable as possible. Ideally, rest periods should be scheduled between test sections. Kids should even be encouraged to exercise by their desks if that will help them blow off steam.

A final caveat: Most parents would not think twice before asking why their local school has scored lower than the national norm. To find out where your school's priorities lie, it might be wise to ask about scores that are consistently higher than the norm as well.

OTHER SOURCES OF INFORMATION

A VISIT TO THE SCHOOL

We have all been in situations where we felt uncomfortable—as though the floor might be pulled out from under us. Obviously, you want your child's educational environment to have a stable, positive "feel." By "being there" at a prospective school, you put yourself in a position to absorb its atmosphere. Moreover, you can learn about it the same way your child will, by using all your senses. From the bulletin boards and class decorations, you can see whether a creative approach to learning is at work. You can hear the way the teachers and principal relate to their students—and to one another. You should feel free to ask any questions that come to you, or question why you don't feel free to do so. Most of all, you can sense whether the school feels good about itself, then decide whether you want your child to share in that feeling.

By now you're getting our message: when you're looking for information, nothing compares with a personal visit. Still, other resources can be helpful—if you carefully consider the source.

A WORD ABOUT WORD OF MOUTH

Because it is *always* subjective, word of mouth must be considered an incomplete source of information. Nonetheless, it can be an excellent way to get to know people's feelings about a school, public or private, if you are careful to get a cross section of opinion.

Begin by asking those closest to you for their input. The friends and relatives who love your child may also share your values. Their opinions may be slanted, but they will be slanted in your child's favor.

Colleagues and friends with whom you share a professional link, but not necessarily the same values, can give you a new perspective on education. And the support or counseling groups you attend singly or as a family (such as Parents Without Partners or Al-Anon) can also be good sources of information. Through their members, you may discover which local schools offer peer counseling or other services that may be of help to your family.

While you are at it, be sure your sample includes families whose children are not yet school age, those whose kids are at that "raging hormone" middle-school stage, and those whose children have gone on to high school. They will let you know which school services you'll need in order to get through the long haul and which may be a temporary need. (Even the best after-school care programs are services children ultimately outgrow.)

Last but not least, pick up as much as you can from those who know the local schools best. What do the teachers who work at the school like and dislike about their jobs? Do room parents, aides, or volunteers have the materials they need? What does the head of the PTO or parents advisory group seem most concerned with: raising money or raising parental consciousness?

And what about the ultimate consumers, the kids? Do they like their school? Their teachers? They may claim they don't, just to save face. But watch them as they head for the bus. Eager, happy kids who can't wait to get to school have been turned on to learning—and that's a turn in the right direction.

AN A FOR EFFORT

In response to skyrocketing school taxes (and increased taxpayer demand for fiscal accountability), many communities are issuing school system "report cards." These informational printouts are offered to all taxpayers currently buying into the school system in hopes that they will come to understand—and approve—what their tax dollars are financing.

The detail of the data varies greatly from community to community. Some offer only scant information: student-teacher ratios, the results of standardized testing, daily attendance records, and perhaps, drop-out rates. Others can net a parent a great deal of information, including the percentage of the district school budget being spent on teachers' and administrators' salaries, a profile of recent public school graduates, comparisons with schools of similar socioeconomic status, and comparisons of test scores with statewide averages.

The school report card is a politically conceived document. It can be rife with double-talk and bureaucratese. In order to read it accurately, you may even have to do some reading between the lines. (For instance, some reports list local scores but no national averages with which they can be compared.) Still, the school report card can give you an overview of the local trends. Check at city hall, your local school department, or the town library for a copy of the local report.

FACTS ON FILE

If, like Dara and Terrence, you are planning to move, or if you are school shopping and need "objective" data,

School-Match, a data base developed by educators, can help you. Offering profiles of *all* U.S. public school systems (plus nearly 8,000 private, parochial, and overseas schools), the typical School-Match listing includes teacher salaries, instructional expenditures, library services, pupil-teacher ratios, and scholastic examination scores. The service is available at many of the larger public libraries.

4
Don't Worry and Other Words of Advice on the First Day of School

"Don't worry." There is no better advice we can offer parents who are sending their children off to school for the first time. And there is no advice more apt to be wiped out of a parent's memory as soon as the first bell rings. And no wonder! With the possible exception of the day your child was born, no other day in his or her life is likely to induce such a confusing hodgepodge of emotion.

There she is, your baby, looking smaller than ever in her "she'll grow into it" school jacket. What if kindergarten turns out to be "too big" for her, as well? What if school is too much for her to handle? Is she mature enough to make a successful separation? What will her teacher say about her abilities as a learner? And finally, *what will it say about your abilities as a parent if your child does not make a successful transition between home and school?*

As educators, we have logged in twenty-plus years of

first-day jitters. In that time, we have watched firsthand as society has steadily increased the pressure to excel on our youngest students. We have seen the first day of school transformed from a bittersweet rite of passage to part one of the Ivy League entrance exam. And we have read the conflict in the faces of the parents who have tried not to think of school as a competitive spot, but who nonetheless want their children to measure up—not only to the challenge of learning but to their peers.

Most parents are able to keep a grip on the temptation to compete. But they may be plagued with nagging questions. Will my son be a kindergarten dropout because he can't sit still? Can a child who lunches daily on white paste really be ready for school? Have we done enough to keep up with the Einsteins? It seems there is no aspect of kindergarten too large or small for a parent to obsess over—beginning with a child's age.

WHAT'S IN A NUMBER

No mistake about it, kindergarten is no longer child's play. What you may have experienced twenty years ago as a glorified day-care center is now real school—and it may be all-day school, at that.

Nor is the average kindergartener an educational neophyte. In fact, he or she is likely to have had two or more years of preschool experience, a great deal of social interaction, and hundreds of hours of letter and number drills gleaned largely from years of watching "Sesame Street." It is no surprise, then, that kindergarten has become increasingly rigorous to meet the demands of its worldly wise charges—and it's so wonder that the magical number five is no longer quite so magical when it comes to ascertaining classroom readiness.

Meg, a single mother, put it this way. "I was always

careful not to rush Devon along—to let her learn at her own pace. I even kept her out of the preschool her neighborhood friends attended just because I felt it pushed reading on kids too early. I always said, 'Wait until you're five. Then you'll be old enough.'

"When she finally turned five and I delivered her to school, I nearly went into shock. The kids in that class weren't just reading and writing—they knew what sushi was! Devon seemed so unsophisticated compared to them! I wanted to take her straight home and wait until she turned six!"

To any parent who has spent four and three-quarter years patiently allowing his child to develop at his own pace, it may seem unnatural to base that same child child's educational entrée on his chronological age. To those well-meaning mothers and fathers who have spent thousands of dollars on early-learning programs in hopes that their kids will get ahead, the age requirements that "keep them back" can seem infuriatingly random. Nor are age requirements any less vexing to school administrators. To compensate for the new, more challenging kindergarten curricula, school systems across the country have moved up their cut-off dates. Yet, although many of these schools have taken pains to exclude all but those children who are solidly five, they may have succeeded only in creating an older group of youngest children. Some school districts in the Midwest have even begun to enroll children on the day of their fifth birthday—whether that birthday falls in September of the kindergarten year of the following May.

So how does a cut-off date function in a child's behalf? Simply, it is a separating mechanism. Since psychologists have learned that "average" five-year-olds (who have usually developed the ability to concentrate, follow directions, and—yes—sit still) are more apt to be successful in kindergarten, an established cut-off date puts school within the reach of those kids who are statistically most apt to handle it. It is expected that if each beginning student has developed the skills he will need to succeed in kindergarten, he will likely be more positively attuned to school throughout his education.

Obviously, "average" five-year-olds come in many varieties. Some are intellectually gifted but may be socially immature. Some are up to a year younger than others and at a physical disadvantage. Some otherwise bright children may be bothered by speech or perceptual difficulties. All these children are normal, active, and interested. Yet they are no more alike than a random selection of the eighteen-year-olds we allow to vote. Whatever your child's age, no number can ever reveal her abilities, pinpoint her needs, or unlock her talents. For that, we must rely on a more personal screening process.

KINDERGARTEN SCREENING: INCLUSION IN ACTION

"I have always been careful not to push Jenny," said Meg, the mother of a school-age daughter. "But when I saw the kindergarten screening announced in the paper, well . . . something just snapped! Suddenly I couldn't just say 'Look at the dogs or the kitty cats,' but 'Look at the *two* dogs or the *four* kitty cats.' It's not that I thought knowing her number was such a big deal, I just couldn't stand the thought of Jenny not getting into school just because she couldn't identify four."

Screening Testing. Admittance. They are powerful words, indeed. And what gives them their power is their ability to remind us of an instance when we were not admitted, when we, as children, did not pass the "test" that would have opened the door to the clique, the in-group, the fun. No parent who has ever felt the sting of being left back or pushed aside doesn't fear the day when her child will be rejected. And that is why it is so difficult to convince parents that the purpose of screening is to identify a child's developmental readiness—not to keep them out of kindergarten. Need proof? Then let's take a peek through the schoolroom door.

At first glance, what you are watching seems to be the classic kindergarten scene: nineteen normal, happy kids grouped around a teacher. But wait. Is this really so normal? Within arm's reach of the teacher's desk are the eager beavers, those students who are busily mimicking what the teacher is demonstrating, sometimes even before she does it. Beyond them sit the "outer circle," boys and girls who clearly get it, but can only muster the gumption to do every other exercise the teacher suggests. On the periphery of the classroom, you may find a group of "kinetics," those antsy five-year-olds who prefer to process information while walking around the room. A few may even be watching the action outside the window.

It is not a scene that inspires great confidence in most parents. Yet, in their own way, all these children *are* learning. They are all achievers. And they have all passed through some screening process.

As we pointed out in Chapter 1, the goal of our public schools is to educate the individual—not to turn students into mirror images of each other. Screening is actually the first step in identifying the personal gifts and individual needs that make each learner special and unique.

The kindergarten screening date is usually announced in the spring or the fall preceding the start of the school year. At that time, you and your child may meet informally with your child's teacher and perhaps a school psychologist, speech therapist, or learning specialist. (If you have already attended an open house or orientation at your child's new school, you have already helped facilitate screening. The teacher will be a familiar face by now.)

Most of the time, the process begins with simple observation. The teacher may watch to see how your child interacts with others. She will look to see whether he turns his head toward a speaker, indicating the possibility of a hearing problem. And as he approaches the desk, she will check his gait for any uneven steps or limp. (They can indicate a muscular or gross motor problem.)

The teacher will then engage the child in casual conversation, listening carefully for any speech problems that may warrant professional help. Five-year-olds love to talk about themselves. Knowing that, the teacher may break the ice by complimenting the child on his "bright green cap," then ask him to identify green—and any other colors he may know—in a box of crayons. If the child knows several colors, she will notes it. If not, she will be sure he learns them during the school year.

Finally, the teacher may ask the child to draw or color a picture so she can check his fine-motor abilities. All the while, she will be making a mental note of the child's attention span and his interest in the interaction.

Ahh, we can see it now: the concerned parents of countless preschoolers, pointing out every possible shade of green with the black tips of their yellow pencils. To them we say, screening is a process, not a test. There are no correct answers—and there can be no failures. Drilling will only open your child up to the possibility of feeling as though she failed *you*.

Instead, try to make your five-year-old feel as comfortable as possible with the screening process. If, for instance, your daughter becomes anxious around strangers, you may need to prepare her. Try to calm her by saying something like, "Your new teacher will be talking to us

66

today. I don't expect to know everything she asks me, and I don't expect you to know everything she ask you."

What if the screening process uncovers a potential problem? Then you can be assured that the process is working! The purpose of screening is to identify a child's strengths *and* weaknesses so that he can be better equipped to succeed. (*Note:* If you suspect that your child has a problem that is affecting his ability to speak or learn, if your pregnancy or your child's birth was especially difficult, or if your pediatrician suggests it, you can request that your child be evaluated as early as age three. Check with your local school board for guidelines and information.) Research has shown us that early intervention—such as speech therapy, physical therapy, or transitional classes—can minimize ongoing learning problems. By providing your young child with the special education services he needs, you enable him to put his best foot forward in kindergarten—and make a positive step toward future learning.

Remember: most kindergartens are prepared to accept a wide intellectual, social, and emotional range of children. It is more than likely that not only will your child be happily enrolled in school, she will flourish! Still, if—by January—you have any remaining question as to her readiness, she can always be rescreened at that time. Chances are, her skills will have improved significantly.

THE QUESTION OF FORMAL TESTING
The mother of a newly enrolled kindergartener told us this story.

As part of the screening process, Ben's new teacher asked him to draw a picture. He finished his creation with aplomb—but a bit too quickly for mother and teacher to get to know each other. To keep him occupied a few minutes longer, the teacher passed him a picture that had been drawn by a future classmate. Ben took the paper. On it was a stick figure sketched in green.

"It's Leonardo," said the teacher. "I'll bet you know who Leonardo is, don't you, Ben?"

Ben paused. "Yes," he answered finally. "Isn't he an artist or an architect or something?"

Certainly, no teacher is curmudgeonly enough to keep Ben from the classroom simply because he couldn't tell a Ninja Turtle from Leonardo da Vinci. It will be a sad day, indeed, when educators expect kindergarteners to glean all their general information from animated cartoons. Yet this is just the kind of answer that can keep a bright child from scoring well on strictly administered entry exams if that particular school uses testing as an exclusionary tool.

Many school systems have developed their own testing instruments. Still, the Gesell School Readiness Test is the entry exam often administered to our five-year-olds. Used by an estimated 20 percent of the nation's school districts, it is given *in part*—along with the kinds of screening methods described above—by many more.

Created in 1925 by Dr. Arthur Gesell, a pediatrician and school psychologist, the test requires children to complete such tasks as naming animals, building with blocks, and filling in a partially drawn stick figure of a man. The child's performance is then compared with a set of age-based norms, and he is scored not with a grade but with a comparative "developmental age." For many kindergarteners, this test may be the sole method for determining readiness.

Recently the Gesell test has come under fire by parents' groups and researchers alike. Comparing a child's achievement against a set of "norms," they argue, is subjective, at best—and may promote ethnic bias, at worst. Whose norms are they, anyway? Do they best serve the interests of foreign-born students who may just be beginning to master the English language? Or are they more likely to benefit the suburban child who has just digested three years of accelerated preschool? An urban child who has just moved to a rural area may not be any more able to identify a cow than our friend Ben—who was not fed a steady diet of cartoons—was able to identify a Ninja Turtle.

This brings us to yet another sticking point: the way the Gesell test—and any other formal test—is used. We, as educators, believe in inclusion. Yet some schools that rely on tests as the sole method of judgment also rely on the tests to give themselves an easy way out. They may use test scores as evidence that a child isn't ready for school when, in truth, the school isn't ready to expand its developmental approach for each child. Others may use such tests to attempt to weed out questionable students before they even reach first grade.

Thankfully, such practices aren't common. But even an erroneous or honest but misguided reading of test results can mean a year-long detour for an otherwise school-ready child. And in school systems that haven't yet adopted the developmental model, that detour often ends at yet another controversial destination: the transitional program.

A PROGRAM IN TRANSITION

In recent years, grouping—the practice of segregating and teaching children according to their academic strengths and talents—has fallen into disfavor. In its stead, many schools have adopted the "developmental model," an individualized teaching method based upon a child's developmental readiness for learning and not his ability to memorize predetermined bodies of knowledge.

Some public schools have accepted the developmental model in toto. Others have adopted many of the more creative aspects of the developmental ideal while maintaining a traditional grade-to-grade structure. Still others are firmly entrenched in a strictly delineated curriculum. It is for the children in these districts, who may not meet the standard social, emotional, or intellectual norms, that the transitional or readiness program was designed.

A typical readiness program prepares a child for all-day school by putting him in a program he *is* ready for—one that he can master. It can be offered either to a prekindergartener who has scored poorly on screening tests or to a child who has completed kindergarten yet is unready to read. The purpose of the program is simple: to offer a young child time to mature so he or she can approach learning with a positive attitude. Ideally, that means keeping class size small (about thirteen to fifteen students) so the child can benefit from one-on-one interaction with the teacher. Such a program should also incorporate a creative, multisensory approach to learning that lets the child "absorb" knowledge in his own way: if he is interested in reading, for instance, he can explore books; if he prefers tactile experiences, he can illustrate what letters stand for while up to his elbows in finger paint. The transition period usually lasts one year.

Some research suggests that that may be one year too many. A number of recently published articles argue against transitional programs, saying that they are just another form of retention. And "staying back" can be a huge blow to a child's developing self-esteem. Badly handled, it can even make a child feel like a failure before his education has even begun.

The National Association for the Education of Young

Children (NAEYC) has taken a firm stand on the transitional issue. It believes that children should not be denied entrance to kindergarten or retained there on the "basis of lack of maturational 'readiness'," that "it is the responsibility of the educational system to adapt to the developmental needs of the children it serves; children should not be asked to adapt to an inappropriate system."

The most precious thing about our kindergarteners is their unabashed uniqueness. It is that uniqueness that is the soul of learning. It is an educator's duty not just to accept each child's individuality but to celebrate it.

Readiness isn't something that comes from a jar (or even from one of those "better baby" programs). It is a natural state your child will achieve *in his own time*. Nevertheless, there is a great deal you can do to enhance your child's readiness—if you are willing to follow your child's lead.

IS THERE SUCH A THING AS UNREADINESS

Yes, there is—and an observant parent can be the first to recognize it.

Most kindergarten teachers expect up to a fourteen-month range in chronological age between their oldest and youngest students. Although the maturational range between students can be even greater, age—some researchers have found—is not in itself a reliable predictor of readiness. In fact, a recent study (by Lorrie Shepard of the University of Colorado and Mary Lee Smith of Arizona State University) has concluded that even the detriment of being the youngest in a class disappears by the third grade *if instruction is individualized*.

Accommodating as it is, however, even the developmental model cannot adequately meet the needs of a developmentally immature child. Therefore, if a kinder-

71

gartener cries daily, if a "slow-to-warm-up" child continues to hug the wall several weeks into the school year, or if the "young" five-year-old finds it a struggle to pay attention, it is worth exploring whether the child might benefit from "the gift of time."

Obviously, no parent should be studying his or her child under a microscope. Still, it is fairly obvious whether or not a child feels "at home" in the classroom. Generally, a well-placed kindergartener will think of himself as a capable individual; he will approach his work enthusiastically; and he will act upon his surroundings, using them to grow in creative thinking, decision making, and problem solving. He will enjoy interacting with his teacher and peers, and, through that interaction, his self-expression will flourish. In short, a fulfilled five-year-old is one whose curiosity and enthusiasm motivate him toward learning.

If your child's teacher suggests that he or she is not making a happy adjustment to school, you may want to step back and reconsider the behavioral signals he or she has been sending. If your son has seemed withdrawn or overwhelmed in play settings or if your child expresses real unhappiness at the prospect of going to school each day, you may want to schedule an appointment with your child's teacher to discuss your concerns.

A word of caution, however: Time is like any other gift. The way it is received has a great deal to do with the spirit in which it is given. There is little evidence that delaying the start of kindergarten is in any way detrimental. In fact, allowing a youngster an extra year to develop has become an increasing trend among many upscale, educated parents. But if you are uncomfortable with the idea of retention or if the gift of time seems more like the theft of a year, your attitude could become a burden to your child. Try to remember that your child's world is his classroom. He will continue to grow and learn whether or not he is in a formal school setting.

DOING WHAT COMES NATURALLY

The proud mother of a new kindergartener accompanied her daughter to her desk. "I'll see you at noon," chirped the parent. "Learn a lot today."

The little girl rolled her eyes. "Oh, for Pete's sake, Mother," she cried, "do I *have* to learn at home and in *school*, too?"

Remember when learning didn't have to involve flash cards or mass memorization or expensive preschool programs? Remember when parents were still too naive to suspect that what the school board was passing off as kindergarten screenings were actually "Kiddie Boards"? Or that a child's ultimate success or failure depended on the honors he had added to his résumé before the age of five? Do you remember when learning was *fun*?

If you find yourself looking back wistfully on those days, we have some good news for you: learning is still—and will always be—a function of a child's natural desire to explore. It began the first time your newborn reached out for a favorite toy. And it will continue as long as your child is encouraged to reach out for knowledge at his own pace, in his own time. You can prepare your child for school and have fun by using the following guidelines:

• *Read to your child.* Did you know that your child can absorb five important lessons in just fifteen minutes a day? He can if you spend those minutes sitting in a comfortable chair browsing through a good book! In the time it takes to read a story, your child can learn that reading is a warm, comforting activity the whole family can share; that "reading" is possible even when you just look at the pictures; that it opens up the imagination and puts the things you are interested in into your hands. Most of all, he will learn that reading is fun. Now, isn't that a whole lot cozier than what he picks up from a flashcard?

- *Get down—and even dirty*. Education is a messy process. And for most kids, that means getting right up to their elbows in whatever they're learning. Let them cover your dining room table with puzzle pieces: later they will use what they've learned to put groups of letters together to make sounds and words. Stock up on finger paints and plenty of paper and let your little Picassos create. Having lots of materials but no teacher around encourages creativity—and allows the child to set his own limits. Even a pail of sand can be an educational toy if a child uses it to build imaginatively. That, after all, is the way the child will build sentences from words and paragraphs from sentences.

- *Use your neighborhood library*. Explore its nooks and crannies the way you would a mysterious, uncharted planet. Let your child lead you through the stacks. It's a good way for you to learn who she is: her likes and dislikes, interests and talents. And get to know your local librarian. He or she can be a wonderful resource.

- *Encourage social interaction before the beginning of school*. Neighborhood play groups teach a child how to get along in a community. Even the most self-possessed preschooler will learn to cooperate when peers—not parents—are setting the limits on behavior. (And she may even coax a neighborhood "big kid" into watching out for her on the first day of school.)

- *Don't make school seem larger than life*. Saying like "Soon you'll be in *real* school" and "You'll have to act like a big boy now!" may foster a fear of failure. Take the stress out of learning by saying instead, "Pencils have erasers because part of learning is making mistakes."

- *Don't use school or the teacher as a threat*. Never say things like "Wait until you start school. Your teacher will punish you for that." Say, rather, "Your teacher is there to help you."

- *Let your child explore the activities he likes, when he likes*. Literature may be something you and your spouse value, but if your five-year-old prefers building blocks to books, let her be! Pushing her toward the activities you prefer will only trample her developing ego. And always allow your child to decide when enough is enough. A bored or stressed child may turn off to learning completely.

- *Don't expect perfection*. Inspired by the alphabet song, little Amy sits down and spends half of her morning at preschool producing a page full of wildly printed alphabet letters. She is so proud she can hardly wait to present her work to her mother. But when her mother arrives, she immediately lets the air out of Amy's balloon. "Oh, Amy, how great!" she says. "But why did you turn those *Bs* around? Remember what I said about the difference between backward and forward? Maybe you'd like to print them for me again—the right way, this time."

It is hard to understand what compels parents—and sometimes teachers—to accentuate the negative. After all, who among us would benefit in any way from having a friend take us aside after a long, hard day to say, "You know that report you gave at work today? Well, don't you think it would have been better if it had been less wordy? Remember we talked about that once before? Well, maybe you'd like to try it again right now."

No matter how well-meaning her mother's criticism, the message Amy received is "What I have done is not good enough. I am a disappointment." And there is little chance that Amy—or anyone else—would be up for a second try after that. Had her mother focused, instead, on the letters she had written correctly, printing would have been an exciting new skill for Amy—not an emotional risk.

• *Encourage your child to share his developing abilities with others.* Show your youngster that what he learns not only is fun but is important to the whole family. Allow your budding mathematician to keep score during family games. You may even encourage your child to send personal thank-you notes for the special gifts he receives. Don't push him to print. Instead, let him draw or color a picture, then send it to the giver. Enlist your friends and relatives in support of your child's education, and he will soon realize how good learning can feel.

SURVIVING THE SCENE AT THE SCHOOLROOM DOOR

It had never occurred to Sharon, the mother of a kindergarten-age daughter, that she would be dealing with first-day-of-school separation anxiety. In anyone's estimation, Jenny was a social dynamo. For all of her five years, she had been the life of every party—and the tickler of the family funny bone. Kindergarten, Sharon thought, would simply provide Jenny with a new audience for her boisterous brand of play. And, for a while, it seemed to be so.

Jenny no sooner came through the kindergarten door than she was off. First, she charmed her teacher. Then she played with some blocks. Then she met a few of her classmates. She even plunked the piano keyboard in passing. Convinced that her gregarious daughter had made another easy adjustment, Sharon turned to go. She had not yet reached the door when she felt a familiar tug at her skirt.

"Oh, hi honey," said Sharon, a little surprised. "You were having such a good time, I didn't think you'd see me leave. Did you want to say just one more good-bye?"

Jenny nodded. Then she turned toward the class. "Good-bye," she called cheerfully. Then she took her mother's hand and led her toward the door—and home.

Every child is born into a completely self-centered world. In that world, an infant comes to know her parents not as individuals or even as people but as the source from which all nourishment, comfort, warmth, and goodness ideally flows. As that child matures, her outlook broadens. Slowly, she begins to know her parents, still not as unique personalities, but for the various roles they play in her life. In happy, functioning homes, these roles include teacher, nurturer, disciplinarian, faithful servant, counselor, playmate. And that is why, when the time comes to loosen the ties that bind, so many children (and quite a few parents) come unglued in the process. Any five-year-old who has always looked to her ever-patient mother for instruction will surely find her teacher—her strange, perhaps preoccupied teacher—a poor substitute. Nor is the youngster who has always played under a caring father's watchful eye likely to be impressed. After all, his dad loved him unconditionally. But his classmates may not even ask him to join in their games!

Nevertheless, the moment your kindergartener takes his first insecure steps over the schoolhouse threshold, he steps into a more peer-oriented phase of life. We like to think of the disconcerting tears that sometimes accompany that step as a sort of "musical fanfare" that heralds in this new period of his or her development. Still, it is important that the crying comes to a timely end. Unless a child makes a happy adjustment to kindergarten—including a natural separation from his parents—he may find himself foundering academically later on, even as late as junior high.

Happily, there is a great deal you can do to bridge the gap between Sesame Street and the neighborhood school—especially if you make an early start.

A HEALTHY SEPARATION STARTS AT BIRTH

Every child is a treasure. Perhaps that's why parents find it so tempting to keep their children as close as they can for as long as they can. But even the most protective couples begin to foster the independence their children will need in order to make it in school—and they often do so without even knowing it.

By arranging for a toddler to stay with a trusted sitter, for example, a parent shows him that time spent away from the family is safe on a temporary basis—and that, no matter where they go without him, his parents will always return. By sending a preschooler to play at a friend's house or by taking advantage of a community day-care center, a parent enables the child to learn that family friends, instructors, and other adults can be trusted to provide nurturance, entertainment, and even fair discipline in a parent's absence.

In fact, even just sending a kid out the door to join in the neighborhood play (or taking part in a play group) can be an educational experience. Surrounded by his friends, a child feels free to act and interact with his peers. And although no parent wants his or her child to become *too* street-smart, the neighborhood is precisely the right milieu for learning one of life's most important lessons: that it is fun to feel like one of the group. Before your eyes, your shy and cautious four-year-old may blossom into a hale and hearty soccer-maniac, not because you've turned blue encouraging him but because "the team needs a goalie." And before you can get out the door to remind your tightfisted three-year-old to share, you may see her handling her precious possessions to a new friend, not because it's the nice thing to do but because the others seem to like her more when she is generous.

Independence is a great responsibility. A child who has learned to take responsibility for her behavior is a child who has learned—in a basic way—some pretty lofty stuff about freedom, self-determinism, and working toward a common good. But she will need a great deal of more down-to-earth information before she can make a successful transition from home to school.

BUT WHERE ARE THE BATHROOMS

Fran had been a quiet, somewhat insecure kind of child. Seeing some of the same hesitancy in her son, Kyle, she took great care to demystify the world for him. When it was time for Kyle to begin his education, for example, Fran led him straight to the elementary school door. From there, mother and son covered every square foot of the building, from the front door to the back, from the principal's office to the cafeteria. Throughout, Fran kept up an exhaustive explanation of nearly every detail of formal education, including how teachers become teachers and who gets picked to clean the blackboards at the end of the day.

By the time the first day of school arrived, it seemed that Kyle knew everything there was to know about his new environment. It came as a great surprise to Fran, then, when Kyle simply refused to take his seat.

"Are you afraid that I'm leaving you?" Fran asked. "I'll be back to pick you up, you know, just like I did at day care. Remember, I showed you where I'd meet you, out by the fence?"

"I remember," Kyle replied with a sob. Obviously, that was not the reassurance he needed. He stuffed his hands into his pockets and stared at the floor.

"Then are you afraid that the teacher will ask you a question that you can't answer?" Fran suggested. "You're here to learn, honey—not to know all the answers."

Kyle bounced a few times on the heels of his new shoes but said nothing.

Finally, Fran took him gently by the shoulders. "What are you afraid of, honey? I can't help you unless you tell me."

Kyle rolled his eyes to the ceiling. "I'm afraid I won't get to the bathroom in time," he whispered anxiously. "I really have to go and you never showed me where it is!"

In the course of our work, we have spoken to countless groups of concerned parents—and thousands of school-age kids. And if we had to characterize the difference between them, we would say this: a parent worries whether his child's reach exceeds his grasp. A kid worries whether or not he is within reach of a bathroom door.

80

To those parents who have invested time, effort, and often a great deal of money in preschool or enrichment programs, this can be disconcerting news. They would prefer that their little scholar spend his days zeroing in on prepositional phrases—not the water closet. Still, an insecure child cannot learn. And, whether we are five or ninety-five, we all experience insecurity when we feel out of place or out of touch with our environment.

Kyle's mother may have overlooked the obvious, but she had the right idea. The best way to make the first day of school comfortable for a child is to make sure it is not, literally, the child's first experience at the school. If your school sponsors an open house or an orientation for in-coming kindergarteners, *go*. Let your child drink from the water fountains, point out the way his heels echo in the hall. Give him a hands-on tour. It'll make him feel that he's in control of his environment. If there is no designated orientation day at your school, ask the school principal whether you might tour the building. And if, in the course of your travels, you encounter your child's teacher, give them a chance to get to know each other. Some parents are so eager to fill a teacher in on a child's talents and abilities that they don't even give the prospective student a chance to talk.

Remember, a child's attitude toward learning is psychologically hereditary: if your son dreads the beginning of school or worries that he won't make friends, he may have "caught" that condition from you. Put the past to rest. Walk your child by the school grounds when recess is in full swing. He'll see for himself that school is neither a dreary place nor a lonely proposition. And when you take him home, *don't make further comment*. It may be tempting to brush first-day jitters aside by saying, "Oh, don't worry. It will be easy," but that just makes it impossible for a child to admit when he's having difficulty. Nor should you anticipate the worst by giving a "this-might-happen-and-that-might-happen" speech. This serves only to make *your* anxiety a part of your child's life—and anxiety is something a parent has plenty of, especially around the first day of school.

WHOSE SEPARATION ANXIETY IS THIS, ANYWAY

No parent intends it, but every teacher has witnessed the following scene: The cool, calm daughter escorts her nervous father to the classroom door. "See you later," she calls. Then she turns to go. Suddenly, the father finds himself groping for his daughter's hand—and for the place he once occupied as king of her attentions. "Do you have your milk money, or do you need some?" he asks, pulling her away from the class. "Maybe we should have packed you a few extra cookies, so you could share with your new friends." Now he is reeling her in like a fish. "Well, have a good day," he adds, now nose to nose with his squirming child. "I hope you don't miss your mother and me *too* much."

Why don't more kids skip blithely off to school? Maybe it's because their parents just can't handle it!

As hard as it is to admit, the family member who is lugging around the separation-anxiety baggage may *not* be the one carrying the Ninja Turtles lunch box. Parents of first-timers, "prepared" parents, even kindergarten good-bye-scene veterans can suddenly find themselves struggling to let go at the schoolroom door. Some are shocked to discover that the child they have always thought of as "the baby" has suddenly come of age—at least in the eyes of the crossing guard. Others may not mind having lost a fledgling from the nest as much as they mind the way the entire nest has been thrown into chaos. (The day school begins, every routine you spent

82

five years developing is suddenly rendered obsolete.) Still others may be reliving their own unhappy first-day memories—or they are simply mired in the emotional paradox of letting go. (No, of course you don't want your child to miss you. But maybe you don't want her to get along *too* well without you, either.)

If the first-day blues are coloring your outlook, you should know that such reactions are common—so common, in fact, that the schools themselves have begun to educate parents on their emotions. In some schools, for example, the principal hosts a coffee hour on the first day. After leaving a child off, each parent is invited back to the cafeteria where he or she can interact with other parents, get reacquainted with the principal, and, perhaps, share feelings. (As any first-day veteran will tell you, you aren't really losing a child; you're gaining an entire class to make cupcakes for.)

Any event held in the cafeteria gives parents a unique opportunity: that is, to feel nurtured by the same school that will be nurturing their children. And because the coffee hour brings the parents of similar-age children together in such a natural way, it also creates an exceptionally fertile environment for networking. The parent-to-parent information exchange can be enhanced further if the school allows parents to put sign-up sheets around the room. Then even those mothers and fathers who leave the kindergarten feeling as though they've lost something can leave the school feeling satisfied. If they've checked the lists, they may have gained a trusted day-care provider, found a new carpool, or discovered a highly recommended after-school care service. They may even have sneaked back (temporarily) into their child's school day as a playground monitor, classroom volunteer, or an aide to their teacher.

Of course, you'll still worry. Teachers, principals, and all rational people *expect* you to worry.

One of the most disagreeable facts parenthood has to teach us is that in real life (just as in school) you can't make a perfect situation for your child. And because of this, no parent ever really stops worrying. Being concerned is your fate. Depending on whom you talk to, it may even be your job.

And what do most kindergarteners' parents worry *about?* The questions listed here are the ones most often asked us. Knowing the answers may not help you sleep nights but may help get you through the next 180 school days.

- *Are preschoolers who enter kindergarten knowing how to add, subtract, or read destined for academic burnout?* There is no child so gifted in so many areas that he cannot be further challenged or enriched. If a child is a natural reader, for example, he should be encouraged to explore the books he loves—and urged to develop the mathematical skills he may not love.

    Surprisingly, many "graduates" of academically accelerated preschools—who may have covered most of the kindergarten curriculum—still have a great deal to learn. Sure, they may have attained computer literacy at the age of four, but a child's emotional and social education takes place largely during periods of "free play." As some research shows, a lack in social skills is as likely to cause an otherwise bright child to fail as is a sense of academic boredom.

    Of course, an attentive parent should always tell the teacher when the classwork has already been covered. But an observant teacher will allow each child the

84

time he needs to make the grade socially and academically.

• *What should I pack in my kindergartener's lunch box?*
This is a question we are asked *every year*. And the answer is not as simple as it seems.

First of all, be sure to put a little love into what your child brings to school. You'd be surprised how much a post-it note with a little smiley face that says "I love you" can nourish a child's self-esteem.

Adults may think of lunch as just a sandwich, but kids think of it as barter. Don't pack up a bag of alfalfa sprouts unless your child's love for them surpasses the probable reaction of his peers. And remember: in the cafeteria, the operative rule is "love my oatmeal raisin cookies, love me." Countless school chums have cemented their friendships over food, so be sure to toss in something a child can share.

• *If immunization is a requirement for school enrollment, why do I keep hearing about an ongoing epidemic of childhood diseases?* Because many parents wait until the last minute before getting their children the shots they need.

In 1990, more than 95 percent of kids had been properly immunized—as required—before enrolling for school. Yet the measles epidemic that continues to sweep the nation is headed for another record year. Moreover, outbreaks of whooping cough (pertussis) and mumps are on the rise.

Inner-city children have historically been the victims of low immunization rates. But since 70 percent of all new measles cases are in unvaccinated infants and preschoolers, U.S. physicians have issued this directive: *all* parents need to vaccinate early (not just in time for school)to give a child's health a shot in the arm.

To protect against the new wave of childhood diseases, the American Academy of Pediatrics recommends the following schedule for childhood immunization:

Two months: DTP (diphtheria, tetanus, pertussis), polio

Four months: DTP, polio

Six months: DTP

One year: tuberculosis test

Fifteen months: measles, mumps, rubella, HIB (Haemophilus influenza type B)* conjugate

Eighteen months: DTP, polio

Four to six years: DTP, polio

Five to twenty-one years: measles, mumps, rubella

Fourteen to sixteen years: tetanus, diptheria

- *Is my child at risk of contracting AIDS?* AIDS can be transmitted only through sexual or blood-to-blood contact. Your child cannot contract AIDS in the course of normal school activities.

And finally,

- *Is there anything a parent can do at home to improve a child's performance in the classroom?* You bet there is—but that answer is a chapter in itself.

---

*The vaccine for Haemophilus influenza type B has now been approved for use in children as young as two months of age. Because the HIB infection is the leading cause of bacterial meningitis, a life-threatening infection of the lining of the brain and spinal cord, and because HIB affects approximately one child in 200, it is important that you speak to your pediatrician about having your child immunized as early as possible.

5
The Home-School Connection

We met Ellen, a neighbor, in the supermarket where she was shopping with her five-year-old daughter, Kristen. She couldn't wait to tell us what they had been up to that day.

"We went to Kristen's kindergarten screening this morning," she enthused. "Not only did we meet the woman who will be Kristen's first teacher, but the principal let us take a peek at her first classroom, too. We got all the firsts demystified in one morning!" Ellen laughed. "Not bad for an hour's work, wouldn't you say?"

Not bad at all—except for a few details. Ellen seemed to forget—as many parents forget—that Kristen met her first teachers five years ago: they were the people who helped her explore the many nuances of warmth, beginning with the day she was born. Her successful screening was not the happy result of "an hour's work." It was formed of five years of love and learning—and of countless patient answers to incessant "whys." Nor can Kristen's first classroom—or any other child's—be found at the neighborhood school. The first seat of learning is and always was the family home.

Home is where the heart of the educational process is. It is the laboratory of applied learning where our youngest "researchers" discover for themselves what happens when one plugs the sink, turns on the water, and leaves the room for an extended period. It is the most fertile of testing grounds where all theories—and the limits of a parent's patience—are tried and tried again. In short, home is where we learn how to learn.

Ask any elementary schoolteacher, and he will run down the methods a child uses to understand and categorize the wildly diverse elements that make up his world. But follow any parent of a curious preschooler for one day, and he will demonstrate them for you. Children learn by active exploration—so parents dutifully plug each electrical outlet with plastic guards. Children learn through inquisition—so parents become masters of explanation, boning up on such critical matters as why the water looks blue in the lake but clear in your hand.

But children also learn by absorption, drawing in all the stimuli around them like sponges. To a curious child, the family home isn't just the classroom—it is the lesson. So why don't more parents realize how much impact their family's life-style can have on a child's learning style?

AN ISSUE OF SECURITY

Norman became a widower at the age of thirty-eight. On that day, he also became a single parent—to his nine-year-old daughter, Julia. Curiously, his relationship with

Julia seemed to flourish when Norman was hitting bottom. Locked in his own grief, Norman stopped being a valuable employee. He even stopped taking care of Julia, who—for a time—became the woman of the house, cooking simple meals, getting herself ready for school, and keeping the house tidy. Somehow, Julia even managed to keep her grades up.

But when Norman changed jobs, sold the family home, and began to date, Julia switched into low gear. "Suddenly, I was getting notes from the teacher telling me that my daughter had become a behavior problem," Norman reported. "Julia was disrupting the class, not turning in assignments . . . and I couldn't understand why. She had gone through the tough stuff like a trooper. But the minute things started to pick up, Julia seemed to fall apart."

As the song says, life goes on. Unfortunately for our children, life can sometimes move along too quickly. Before the kids know what hit them, their parents have changed jobs, gotten laid off, moved, divorced, remarried, and perhaps moved again. Nor is this kind of abrupt change the exclusive domain of the single-parent family. Two-career families are frequently families-in-transit. Working mothers with one foot on the corporate ladder and the other in the laundry room struggle to maintain their balance. Increasingly, the typical American family is a harried and hassled family. For them and their children, home may not be that quiet eye in the center of the storm but an endless blur of comings and goings, where there is never time to memorize one another's schedules, never mind the multiplication tables.

But family life can be made a little more secure for each of us—and all it takes is a little time and some organization.

WHAT'S SO SPECIAL ABOUT QUALITY TIME

We've all done it. In our rush to be caring parents, loving mates, and successful professionals (all at the same time), we've given each of those roles shorter shrift than we would like. And because it seems that there is so little of us to go around, we may find ourselves doing what we vowed we'd never do: giving that homework check less than our total concentration, listening vacantly to a child's story, or simply wondering whether or not there really is such a thing as "quality time."

Television has always painted "meaningful" family time with a broad brush and rosy paint. That's why so many of us think of quality time as something that happens only in sane, sedate, fictional families, like the one headed by June and Ward Cleaver. To those of us who occupy more "lived in" households, just calming the din long enough to find out where everybody is can be as impractical as wearing pearls to do the dishes.

But real time (and real life) doesn't have to stop in order for quality time to exist. Nor do you have to be in a special place to touch base with your children. Quality time happens anytime you establish an emotional connection with your child. Once the connection is made, any activity can seem quite special: from flipping through the yellow pages to flipping burgers on the grill.

"But I'm tired after work," one parent protested. "And besides, I still have all the household chores to do." No problem. If you're cooking, hand your child the spatula. With that simple gesture, you have brought your child meaningfully into your world where she can share your thoughts and your responsibilities. Watching the news? Use it as an opportunity to discuss current events. In fact, if you think of time as a valuable commodity that you can share with your child, even running errands can be a quality experience, as the father of a son in primary school recently showed us. He brought his young son to the bank and, taking about three minutes, actually showed him how to use an ATM card. The father may learn to regret it once his son is using that ATM to stock up on designer jeans, but the whole episode brought them closer together in a way even a television scriptwriter would envy.

SHARING TIME—IN SEPARATE HOMES

Current estimates are that 60 percent of today's marriages will end in divorce. By the end of the decade, approximately half of our nation's children will have experienced the breakup of their parents' marriage. For many of these children, the divorce will be just the first in a series of major life changes. Seventy-five percent of their mothers and eighty percent of their fathers will remarry in three to five years (often while the child is still fantasizing that the parents will get back together).

Nor is remarriage likely to mark the end of the changes for the child of divorced parents. He may have to move out of the family home. He may undergo a change in schools, a change of friends, or a change in economic status. And no matter how custody is divided, he may find himself in a nearly constant state of transit. For many of these children, divorce means constant shuttling between school, preschool care, after-school care, weekends with grandparents, visits with relatives, and two separate households. In a week they may be asked to adapt to as many as six different environments, each with its own set of rules and regulations.

If the ideal home is a secure place where creativity and learning are fostered, then the shared-custody situation is—at least potentially—its undoing. Granted, amicably shared custody is still the best our legal system (and two loving parents) can do for a child under such difficult circumstances. (Although one Massachusetts judge actually ordered the child to remain in the family home while her parents moved in and out, simply to protect her right to the security of a full-time home.) In not-so-amicable cases, some children depend on the school to give them the stability they don't get at home. Others use the school as a safe place to fall apart, emotionally and academically.

Single parents cannot be in all places at all times. And blended families don't always blend thoroughly. These are the facts of divorced life. But your public schools are prepared to patch some of the gaps between home and school—if you, as parents, can patch up your differences long enough to alert them to your situation.

It may not seem like much to you, but an offhand statement like "Take this paper home and show it to Mommy" is a painful thing to hear when there is no Mommy in the home. Tell your child's teacher about your impending divorce. It will sensitize her to the situation. And seeing the teacher accept the separation may help your child to accept it as well.

The chaos of divorce may give your child the feeling that no one is looking out for him. Reinforce his sense of security by staying in the know about school functions. Most schools will gladly arrange to have both the custodial and noncustodial parents notified simultaneously by mail of any school situation that needs parental attention.

In those cases where the separation is the result of a family dysfunction (like alcoholism, drug abuse, or battering) and treatment is being sought, the principal, teacher, and the school psychologist all need to be informed. A child who has been exposed to such behaviors can act out his confusion in a number of unacceptable ways. Letting the authorities know about the situation ensures that your child will be treated as a recovering codependent—and not as a behavior problem.

Finally, every parent—divorced or not—should make certain that school officials know whenever a major life change is in the offing for his or her child. It is perfectly understandable that divorcing parents (or those who are coping with difficult family problems) may be hesitant to air their private affairs in school. Still, by telling the appropriate professionals, you can create a safety net at home and school to support your child through the transition period. If the idea of confiding in school authorities still bothers you, think of it this way: you'd tell the school nurse if your child had chicken pox. It's only fair that you alert the appropriate people when he is confronting other problems.

THE LAST-MINUTE SECURITY CHECK

Enabling a child to learn means empowering him to make sense of the world around him. By providing a safe, secure home environment for your child, you provide him with a stable base from which he can explore the world around him and the ability to act upon what he has learned in a creative way. To be really secure, your child must know that you are in control of every aspect of his life, and that your dedication to his protection is as tangible as the roof over his head. The security checklist that follows may strike you as being made up of the most mundane kind of information—but this is the stuff security is made of. If your answers to some of these checkpoints are shaky, it may be time to take the necessary steps to remedy this situation.

CHECKLIST FOR PARENTS

	Yes	No
I know the name of my child's teacher, the school principal, school psychologist, and school nurse	___	___
I know the route my child takes to the school or bus stop	___	___
I know the number of the bus my child takes to and from school	___	___
My child knows and understands the bus rules	___	___
I arranged for someone to care for my child until the school day begins	___	___
I told my child what to do if he gets sick on the way to school	___	___
I told my child what to do if she leaves her lunch or an assignment at home	___	___
If there is an emergency dismissal at school, my child knows where to go	___	___
I provided school personnel with my work phone number as well as the names of phone numbers of relatives or neighbors who can be reached if I am not available in case of an emergency	___	___
I always send a note to my child's teacher after she has been absent	___	___
I notified the school authorities about any special health problems my child has	___	___

Your children will feel better if you have educated them about the safest way to travel to and from school.

The following checklist will educate them (and you) about the finer points of their security.

CHECKLIST FOR CHILDREN	YES	NO
I know several important phone numbers, including my parents' work numbers, the school number, and the emergency services number	____	____
I know how to use a public telephone and always carry correct change	____	____
The safest place for me is with a group of friends. I will never go off alone, even to make an emergency telephone call	____	____
I always take the same route to and from school. Shortcuts or detours through nearby woods are not safe for me	____	____
If a public phone is not nearby and I need an adult's help, I can go to a special neighbor designated by my parents, whom I can trust to help me in their absence	____	____
I know who will pick me up if I am sick	____	____
My parents and I have chosen a secret word. I am not allowed to go with anyone who comes to pick me up unless that person knows the secret word	____	____

WHEN MOM CAN'T BE THERE . . . A GUARDIAN ANGEL FOR YOUR CHILD

Your public school is just as concerned about your child's safety as you are. In order to verify the absence of a child and be certain about his whereabouts, many elementary schools have instituted "guardian angel" or safety programs. When a child is going to be absent, a parent calls the school office and relays the information either directly to the school secretary or through an answering machine that has been hooked up specifically to take these messages. The school secretary then phones the homes of those children whose absences have not been reported.

Time-consuming? Terribly. Necessary? Wouldn't we all like to know if the child we sent out the door in the morning did not arrive in school? If your school doesn't offer a similar program, we recommend that you implement one. The guardian angel program is not free, but the cost can be minimized if the calls placed from the school are made by parent volunteers. Certainly, the feeling of security it brings parents justifies the cost of an answering machine.

STRESS: THE BREAKFAST OF CHAMPIONS

Robert, an advertising executive, had just dropped his three children off at school. He leaned out of the car window. "I can't explain it," he shrugged. "As soon as the alarm goes off, the kids start to argue. I'm pushing my daughter into the bathroom and she's saying, 'But Robbie stole my toothbrush. How am I supposed to get ready for school without a toothbrush?'

"Meanwhile, my son is sitting at the kitchen table refusing to eat. My wife is pulling her hair out. When the bus comes, nobody's ready. The next thing I know, I'm driving everybody to school. They're in the back seat, battling all the way."

Robert laughed. "The young turks get to the office raring to go. By the time I get to work, I feel like I've been through a war!"

By the time the last child is shooed out the door, many parents *have* been through a war. While TV families toast the new day with steaming cups of Ovaltine, real kids have to be nagged to get up, begged to eat up, exhorted to hurry up, and sometimes cautioned to shut up dozens of times before they begin to search for their "lost" shoes.

That's when the coaxing begins. "Do you have your lunch money?" "What is your homework doing in the oven?" "You have gym today. Where are your sneakers?" It is as though our children's minds are self-cleaning and every detail they have ever committed to memory has somehow been summarily erased. Except for those things you really wish they'd forget: like the list of terrible names they call their siblings.

There's no doubt about it: morning tension takes its toll on us—and on our children. One teacher we spoke to said that she can tell immediately which children start each day with a jolt of anxiety. By the time they get to school, they're either too keyed up or too emotionally drained to get down to learning.

We all have days that we'd rather spend under the covers. But you can get your children off to a smoother start if you consider these suggestions.

- *Be there*. Or make sure a trusted caregiver is there to offer guidance to your children. It is always surprising to us just how many school-age kids are expected to get up and out every morning by themselves. If you must leave the house before your children, find a decent before-school care program to provide a transition between home and school.

- *Take time to organize your own life*. A hassled, harried parent who gathers up his stuff in ten seconds and charges out the door with one shoe on is apt to have kids who blast off the same way. Set a good example, and you are giving your children a safe, secure timetable to fit their activities into.

- *Make rules and then stick by them.* Have a daughter who dawdles over breakfast? Keep her toys out of reach until breakfast is eaten, and she'll finish her meal in record time.

- *Simplify chores.* Let kids hang their pajamas on wall-mounted hooks rather than jangly hangers. Invest in fuss-free bedspreads that just have to be pulled up to look neat. Let them toss scattered toys into a toybox. Mornings can be a lot more relaxing if we are willing to relax our standards just a little bit.

- *Be sure you have shown your kids exactly what will satisfy your expectations.* For example, you can't expect your son to dress himself correctly if you haven't taught him that the shirt label goes on the inside. Nor will your daughter leave the bathroom tidy if you haven't shown her which rack to hang her towel on.

- *To stop fashion arguments before they start, allow your child to make a choice about what she wears.* Every child needs to feel that she has control of her personal style. If she tends to equivocate, limit her choice by laying out two outfits from which to choose. Giving a child the right to choose enables her to feel better about the morning routine.

And don't criticize when a fashion experiment bombs. When we see a child come to school ablaze in stripes and plaids, or with his shirt on inside out, we always comment positively. He may look a fright, but nothing goes together more naturally than education, creativity, and a growing sense of independence.

- *Get your child an alarm clock*. Many kids react more positively to an alarm than to their parent's nagging voice.

- *Be firm with chronic bus-missers*. Make it clear that, if your child misses the bus, you will take her to school *once*. If she is late after that, she will have to pay the school penalty.

- *Don't serve hated foods for breakfast*. If you knew you had to face a smorgasbord of your least favorite dishes, how eager would *you* be to get up?

- *Develop a bedtime routine*. Lay out clothing for the morning, go over homework, and deal with any permission slips your child needs you to sign. Keep to the bedtime you have set. But let the last thing between you and your child be a little TLC. Your child's bedtime should not be treated like business.

ACTIVITIES IN OVERDRIVE

Ten minutes into the PTO meeting, Elizabeth was already yawning. ''I don't know about you, but I'm beat,'' she confided to the mother next to her. Her neighbor laughed. Then she commented that undereye circles were the mark of a busy mother.

''Busy mother, nothing,'' Elizabeth corrected. ''Busy kid, is more like it! Between modern dance, Brownies, and piano lessons, Susan has something scheduled for every night of the week. Her schedule is running me ragged!''

Nothing affects a morning like what went on the night before—and for increasing numbers of children, every night is organized activity night. On Monday, it's Scouts.

Tuesday, it's tennis. Wednesday, Thursday, and Friday go by in a blur of meetings and lessons. Even on Saturday, there's no sleeping in. The entire family goes to the unisex soccer league.

We all breathe a sigh of relief when we can get our children away from the television and on to something a bit more productive. Besides, extracurricular activities, we have heard, can help a child develop self-esteem. But if your child's after-school life is exhausting you, it is undoubtedly exhausting him. And you can't expect a child to catch up on his sleep or keep up with the class when he hardly has time to catch his breath!

Any child, no matter what age, must have at least two open, unstructured afternoons for informal or neighborhood play. Otherwise, he or she is in danger of being overscheduled. And that can affect more than the family's schedule.

MAKING UNSTRUCTURED TIME WORK FOR YOU

How do you feel when every minute of every day is set up for you? What's the one thing you want? Time to be alone, to listen to music, read, people-watch, or just loaf. It shouldn't surprise you that your kids might need a little free time as well.

"But just hanging around is such a waste!" complained one well-meaning mother. "When Barry has nothing to do, he does nothing!" But is that really a fair assessment? To us, a kid with time on his hands is like a kid with paint on his hands: you may not be sure what he's been creating, but it's a sure sign he's been creating something! Imaginative thought may not be welcome in structured group activities. It tends to create havoc. But free time offers a child the opportunity to explore the world around him at his own pace and to fill his time as he sees fit. He may use that time to get to know the older and younger people in his neighborhood (an antidote to organized activities since they tend to group children by age). He may use it to get to know the rules of behavior that will make him an accepted member of the community (an antidote to the rules and regulations imposed by coaches and instructors). Most of all, he will use his free time to explore his own creativity because there won't be a coach there to tell him when to take the next step, and there won't be a teacher there to tell him how to fill his time.

As we said before, today's families are especially harried. In fact, there are families who are so harried that anything "disorganized," or any random event, seems to throw them out of whack. Perhaps that—and the fear that their kids aren't getting a well-rounded "childhood experience"—is why kids just aren't spending time making cloud pictures anymore.

If we could, we would ask every parent of an over-scheduled child to examine his or her motivation for so much structured activity. Is your child taking soccer because you are a failed athlete? Are you ignoring his interest in dance because it doesn't fit into your macho mentality? Are you overenrolling him to make yourself feel like a better parent—or to get him out of the house so *you* can have some free time?

The bottom line is this: if our children spent more time discovering themselves, they might spend less time stumped by art projects or creative-writing assignments. And perhaps if we, as parents, spent more time examining our own motivations, our kids wouldn't have to fend us off with excuses like "I don't feel well" or even "Can't I just stay home and do my homework?"

Martin was a bright, fun-loving first grader whose interest in dinosaurs made him the classroom expert on prehistoric life. When anyone wanted to know what a stegosaurus might eat for breakfast or what color to color a pterodactyl, Martin was the one to ask. Suddenly, just a few months into the year, Martin's schoolwork began to slack off. The day science projects were due, he came in empty-handed, even though he had been working on an elaborate dinosaur battle scene only a week before.

The teacher asked Martin if he had had a problem with the assignment.

"My father says that I get too much homework for a first grader," Martin announced. "If you try and make me do it, he'll take me out of this school."

They can be willful and they can be exasperating, but most of the time, children do what they believe will please us. Although no one wants his or her child to grow up to be an approval junkie or a Stepford Child, it is appropriate for parents to reward good behavior. By reinforcing acceptable behaviors, we are instilling in our child the qualities she will need to become a disciplined student, a reliable friend, and a healthy, functioning member of the community.

But healthy, independent responses don't always please all parents. And a grade-*A* report card may *not* make Papa proud—particularly if Papa barely passed the same class thirty years earlier.

To some extent, we are all guilty of passing on our classroom prejudices to our children. We expect them to excel in those courses that we excelled in (as though our personal interests are passed to our children in their

DNA). We shrug off their below-average performances by saying, "Oh well, like mother like son." In some families, failure in certain subjects is actually passed down through the generations like grandma's silver.

In many ways, Martin's father was a dinosaur, himself. His deep-seated feelings about homework (and possibly teachers) kept him locked in the past. His prejudices even threatened his son's natural curiosity with extinction.

What emotional baggage of yours might your child be carrying to and from school? The following subject inventory can help you reflect on the events that shaped your relationship to learning—and the attitudes that may be shaping your child's today. Simply check "pro" if you liked the subject and "con" if you did not. Then take a minute to consider your answers. If you have strong negative feelings about a subject or the teacher of that subject, your past may be affecting your child's future.

SUBJECT	PRO	CON
Reading	——	——
English	——	——
Math	——	——
Science	——	——
Social Studies	——	——
Spelling	——	——
Book reports	——	——
Homework	——	——
Physical Education	——	——
Music	——	——

Art	___	___
Conduct	___	___
Recess	___	___
Lunch	___	___
School Principal	___	___

Just as parental attitudes can affect a child's zest for learning, so too can the following common household hazards.

A NEW DEFINITION OF HOMESICKNESS

John and Leah had scrimped and saved for years before they could afford the home of their dreams: a large Victorian with room enough for their three children. But when John began to remove the layers of old paint from the vintage woodwork, the family came up against a frightening problem.

"I first noticed the change in our four-year-old, Kate," said Leah. "She began to complain of headaches. And when I asked her questions, she sometimes seemed confused, as though she really couldn't remember what happened yesterday."

"When the doctor tested her blood and urine and diagnosed her with lead poisoning, I told him flat-out that he had to be wrong," John added. "I was always careful not to leave chips of lead paint lying around."

"But the doctor told us that Kate got sick by breathing in the lead particles in the air. The same air we had *all* been breathing! That's when we really went clean-up crazy," explained Leah. "After all, if you can't feel safe in your own home, where can you feel safe?"

Where, indeed? While we were busy having our collective environmental consciousness raised, the Environmental Protection Agency (EPA) released the disturbing news that the indoor air pollution that contaminates our homes can be up to five times higher than outdoor pollution—even for those living in nonindustrial, countrified surroundings! And of the 150 common indoor contaminants identified by the EPA, lead has become the number-one toxic waste problem for children.

It is common knowledge that small amounts of lead paint, swallowed before the age of six, have a direct impact on a child's brain and nervous system (and, therefore, on learning). Now it is discovered that lead paint dust, such as the type created by renovating or paint removal, is equally dangerous when inhaled, especially by preschoolers whose livers are not yet fully able to detoxify poisons.

Because of the resurgence of interest in the renovation of older homes by young families, it has been estimated that lead may be contaminating as many as 60 million homes—and up to 25 percent of all American children. *It is critical that these children—and any others at risk—be tested and treated.* Even a slight case of lead poisoning can cause behavioral changes, short-term memory loss, and slow a child's mental development. In extreme cases, a child may suffer seizures, weakness, confusion, and brain and nervous system disorders severe enough to put him years behind his peers in school.

The Environmental Protection Agency has cited some 150 toxic chemicals—including asbestos, radon, formaldehyde (often used in new drapes, carpets, and particle board), and pesticides—that are commonly found in typical households. If you suspect that indoor contaminants may be impairing your child's ability to learn (some symptoms are similar to those of certain learning difficulties) or if your children are suffering from headaches, nausea, rashes, mood swings, sleep disorders, or a marked decrease in mental acuity, contact your doctor immediately. Then contact the EPA or your local environmental group for tips on how to clean up safely.

TOXIC FAMILIES

That millions of children each year are subjected to sexual abuse, physical violence, or emotional battering is a national tragedy. But the fact that, more often than we care to admit, our most innocent citizens experience these atrocities at the hands of those who are duty-bound to nurture and love them is perhaps our greatest human shame.

Toxic families come in many varieties. In some, the abuse is meted out physically or sexually. In others, the children fall victim to chronic neglect or emotional battering. Still other toxic families are headed by parents whose dependency on illegal drugs or alcohol has led them to abuse or neglect those who are most dependent on them. But no matter what form it takes, the toxic lifestyle is a truly poisonous situation. Its effects can taint a victim's life well into adulthood. And whether the abuse is physical or emotional, whether the scars are visible or invisible, all abuse is devastating to the developing psyche of a young child.

THE HARD LESSONS OF CHILD ABUSE

Andy was a second grader who had been physically abused by his father, who no longer lived with the family. Unfortunately, living with Andy was almost too much to bear for his emotionally unstable mother. The fact was, the boy looked a lot like his father. That made Andy an obvious target for his mom, who never failed to remind him that he was ''just like his no-good father.''

Andy spent a good deal of time complaining to his teacher about falls he had taken in the schoolyard—falls that no one ever seemed to witness. He frequently asked to see the school nurse so that he could get Band-Aids for his scrapes.

When Andy began to struggle in school, an evaluation was done to ascertain whether he had a problem that made learning difficult. What the evaluation revealed, however, was that Andy was being emotionally abused. His family dynamics were affecting his ability to learn.

Soon, school personnel were able to see Andy's curious playground behavior for what it really was: a young boy's attempt to put a Band-Aid on a painful situation. There was nothing he could do to get some TLC at home, but all he needed was a scratch to get some at school.

Child abuse, in the long run, is an abuse of authority. Because they are essentially powerless, children must rely on the adults around them to provide them with everything they need, including food, love, guidance, affection, security, and companionship. When a child is traumatized or maltreated, an essential building block of his personality—his ability to trust—is shattered.

Volumes have been written describing the ways the symptoms of physical, emotional, or sexual abuse may manifest themselves in childhood behavior. With more than one million children abused annually by their parents alone, nearly any elementary schoolteacher could add chapters to the existing literature. All she would have to do is draw upon the way these symptoms play themselves out daily in our classrooms.

A physically abused child may be very aggressive or extremely withdrawn. She may appear frightened of her parents and balk when asked to deliver a message from school to home. She may flinch when approached or touched, especially by an adult. A battered child may offer well-thought-out but totally unbelievable explanations for any visible bumps and bruises, either in an attempt to protect her abuser or in an effort to deny to herself that the abuse is ongoing. The physically abused child may even be teacher's little helper, offering to clean the blackboard, tap the erasers, or do anything that will give her a reason to avoid going home.

A neglected child is one who is not having his basic needs met. He frequently arrives at school without a lunch or lunch money. He may hint at being left alone for extended periods—or he may brag about it. At the end of the day, the neglected child may not seem to have anyplace to go. You may see him wandering the halls, playground, or the streets. And because bedtime has little meaning in a family where even mealtimes are ignored, the neglected child may lack physical stamina. He may even fall asleep in school.

Emotional abuse takes many forms—and so do its consequences. The abusing parent may lack parenting skills and, therefore, resort to name-calling, belittlement, or manipulation to bully a child into submission. A "quiet" parent may also be an emotional abuser if she reacts to unacceptable behavior by withdrawing in anger or giving her confused children "the silent treatment." Caught up in that kind of emotional push-pull, the child might become aggressive—or he might take a lesson from his parents and withdraw in order to protect his developing ego from further damage.

For one out of every three girls and one out of every seven boys, sexual abuse—at the hands of a father, step-

108

father, uncle, brother, grandparent, stranger, or even a teacher—is a devastating fact of life. Nor does the trauma end when the abuse stops. Being touched or being forced to touch others in a sexual way can prompt a child to emotionally regress to an earlier (perhaps preabuse) age. It can cause a boy or girl to shrink from human contact— or to display sexual knowledge and behaviors that are inappropriate for his or her age.

A child's behaviors are barometers that can tell us how she is weathering her home and school life. Obviously, a dramatic change for the worse in academic or social skills should never be taken as evidence of abuse. Considering how shocking some of the symptoms of child abuse can be, it may be hard to understand how a parent can overlook them. But abuse doesn't happen in a vacuum. And within the toxic family, where dysfunction is the norm, it can be difficult to see a child's sickness for the sickness around her. One family psychologist compared searching out the root problem in severely dysfunctional families to tracking down a cough in a tuberculosis ward.

But the child's teacher is immune from that "family disease." Furthermore, because of her training and experience, she is familiar with the range of behaviors appropriate to children of a certain age. And that is why a teacher is very often the first person to pick up on the child's signals when something isn't right.

HOW THE SCHOOL STAFF CAN HELP

What happens at home should *stay* at home . . . that's what our parents always told us. And in the context of a functional family, it is to everyone's advantage that a child learn to be discreet. But secrecy is a weapon that abusers use to silence their victims. And silence is the ultimate barrier to emotional healing. As psychologists tell us, our dysfunctional behaviors don't die: they are passed down from parent to child like a dark, unspeakable family legacy. It is critical, then, that we break the silence—and the cycle of abusive behavior.

Still, it *is* threatening to have our children "telling tales out of school," especially when they're doing it *in* school. We may not like the idea of a counselor or school psychologist meddling in our problems (particularly if we live in a tightly knit but not tight-lipped community). We may fear that a child who independently seeks help is a child we cannot control. We may be concerned that the psychologist has usurped our role as the child's main source of help. In extreme cases, we may simply fear losing a child to foster care. But deeply ingrained family problems can hang around so long they can seem like part of the furniture. Your child may need someone to be on his side and to look at his family situation with a fresh eye. In school that someone is his counselor or the school psychologist.

The counselor and the school psychologist are uniquely qualified to act as advocates on a child's behalf. They both have bachelors degrees, though not necessarily in the fields of education or psychology. In addition, the school psychologist has at least a masters degree and may be certified, either regionally or nationally. Since certification requires additional training beyond the masters level, a two-year practicum, and the periodic upgrading of knowledge, you can be sure that any information or advice she offers you is based on the most current research.

But make no mistake about it: the job of the school staff is to advocate *on your child's behalf*. If a child's behavior has become a danger to himself or to others, or if his grades are bottoming out, the school staff will summon the child's entire support system—family and school—for a meeting. If the problem involves the entire family—like alcoholism, for example—the psychologist or counselor will recommend whatever mode of treatment she feels will best benefit the child—including group therapy. But school psychologists, principals, and teachers are not in the business of protecting environments they consider to be abusive. They are mandated to be reporters, charged by the state to report every suspected case of abuse or neglect to the proper authorities. At the same time, however, school counselors and psychologists are parents and family members, too. They understand the demands of daily life—and how crucial it is that a healthy home-school partnership remain intact for the sake of the child.

Melissa was now in the third grade. Her parents began fighting when she was still in the second grade. Somehow the little girl was able to keep it all together as long as the family remained in the same house. But shortly before Christmas, the problems reached a crescendo and Melissa's father decided to move out.

For the next month, Melissa steadfastly refused to discuss the situation with either her mother or her father. But just when it seemed as though the girl was in deep denial, and that her stoicism was taking its toll emotionally and academically, Melissa's mother contacted an old ally: Ms. Pacheco. Ms. Pacheco had taught Melissa in the first grade and remained her favorite teacher.

"By the way, Melissa," her mother mentioned, "I saw Ms. Pacheco in the schoolyard today—and I told her that Daddy and I are getting a divorce. I just wanted you to know that if you want to talk to her about it, it's fine with me."

It took several weeks, but Melissa finally did approach

her favorite teacher. And although it didn't make the divorce any easier to swallow, it did help her to talk about it.

Who do you go to when you need someone to lend an ear—or a shoulder to cry on? Many of us look for someone who may have experienced a similar problem, someone who has walked in our shoes and can legitimize our feelings. Some of us seek out a trusted friend with whom we share values, goals, and perhaps a history. And nearly all of us look for someone who is not a part of the problem to suggest a reasonable solution. With your help, your child can find someone with all those qualifications—as Melissa did—right on the school staff.

In many school systems, the psychologist visits each classroom to explain her role in the school. She may introduce herself by saying something like, "I am a friend of your principal and your teacher. You all know what the principal does: he's the boss. And your teacher helps you learn new things. But do you know what I do? My job is to make sure that you are happy and that school is a happy place for you. If school is not happy, I hope that you will feel free to talk to me." At that time, she may also set up a system that enables children to contact her confidentially, perhaps by leaving a note in her office mailbox.

There is no need to feel threatened if your child approaches a trusted teacher or psychologist alone. Honesty is essential to your child's emotional health and the well-being of your family.

If yours is a family under stress, or if you feel that you are yelling too much, spanking too hard, or losing control too often, you need to blow off steam—and so does your child. Encourage him to speak to a teacher he trusts. It will keep him from feeling isolated, help him to get in touch with his feelings, and make it possible for healing to begin. And be sure to set an example by seeking help yourself.

We all have a moral obligation to report child abuse if we know, or suspect, that it is happening. But fulfilling that obligation can become a trauma in itself if the abuser is your spouse, relative, or family friend. How can a nonabusive parent protect her child when she is being abused as well? What steps should a parent take if he suspects that his child is being abused?

- *Believe your child.* In order to tell you about the abuse, your child had to overcome her fear of the abuser, her own denial, and the possibility that she would be blamed, ridiculed, shunned, or abused again for her trouble. Don't let your denial get in the way of her treatment. Take her at her word.

- *Recognize your role in the problem.* "I don't hit Steven," one defensive mother said. "My husband hits Steven—and me, too." The dysfunctional family is an ongoing drama, and each member in it has his role to play. Although you may not be the actual abuser, you may be his enabler: that is, the person who makes it possible for him to abuse. If you find yourself making excuses for a violent spouse ("You shouldn't have made Daddy angry, dear") or if you have stopped being a parent because you, too, are a victim, you may be playing out of a role in the family drama that is damaging to your children.

- *Get your priorities straight.* Many battered women stay

in abusive relationships in order to "preserve the marriage." Your first priority must be the safety of your children.

• *Make your children safe*. Sexual or physical abuse batters a child's self-esteem. If you can't keep your children safe at home, you must remove them from the home.

• *Stop perceiving help as a threat*. Whether you are the abuser or the nonabusive parent, an addict or codependent, or if you simply recognize any of these tendencies in yourself, you must seek help—for your children's sake.

It costs nothing to reach out for guidance. Here are some toll-free numbers that can put you—and your family—on the path to healing.

> Al-Anon Family Group Headquarters: 800-356-9996
> National Center for Missing and Exploited Children: 800-843-5678
> National Child Abuse Hotline: 800-422-4453
> National Cocaine Hotline: 800-262-2463
> Parents Anonymous: 800-421-0353

6
Everything I Ever Needed to Know I Learned at the Playground

All work and no play make Jack and Jill less sensitive to their peers, less attuned to their relationships, and less well prepared for life, according to social scientists. That's because what goes on in the school playground is *not* just child's play—it is a critically important part of the education process. Kids may master spelling in the classroom, but they learn all they know about fair play, competition, loyalty, and tolerance for individual differences on the playground. And they learn it from the hardest teachers of all, their peers.

Because they are inclusive, your public schools are the ideal laboratory for your child to experiment safely with socialization. There, your son can really indulge himself in modeling play, simply because there are so many kinds of people to model himself after. And there, your daughter can hunt through her environment like a young explorer, knowing that no matter how far she goes in her own imagination, she is still learning under a teacher's watchful eye.

What your child mainly learns on the playground is how to make a friend and be a friend. On the surface, that may seem a rather simple goal. But it is this kind of enduring life-lesson that will carry him well into adulthood and enhance every relationship he has along the way.

SOCIALIZATION: THE ULTIMATE EXTRACURRICULAR ACTIVITY

Friendliness—that sense of open amiability that makes a child approachable—seems to come more naturally to some youngsters than to others. We have all seen the way an unabashedly gregarious child simply takes a potential playmate captive, grabbing her by the hand and pulling her into play.

But socialization—the ability to adapt to the common needs of a social group—is an acquired skill. Whether a child is reticent or rowdy, whether she is more of a maniac or a brainiac, every child can become a valued member of her peer group as long as she is willing to learn the rules of social behavior and play by them. Best of all, the same rules that get a kid through the third-grade social whirl will help him get along with professional colleagues and bosses later on.

What can we hope our children learn from play? And how can we help them learn to play fairly? We can start by reinforcing important lessons like the following:

BE A GOOD SPORT

What if your boss dropped by your office tomorrow and said, "I know you've outperformed Joan. I know that you're a better employee than Joan. But I want you to know that I'm giving the promotion to Joan because we can pay her less money." It may not be pleasant, but it's common business practice. It is also common playground practice—the kind that gives the innocence of youth a black eye.

Admit it: sportsmanship has its downside. Good guys sometimes *do* finish last. A gracious loser still feels sore. And the fastest runners don't get picked first for the relay race team if the lousy runner happens to be "cooler."

But if good sports are not born (and they are not—kids hate to lose!), they still can be made, especially if a parent takes some pains to take some of the pain out of losing.

Don't just give lip service to slogans like "It doesn't matter whether you win or lose—it's how you play the game." That kind of philosophizing doesn't mean much to a child. If losing brings out the worst in your son, guide him toward co-operative activities in which there are no clear-cut winners or losers. Or, if you can control the outcome of the games you play, let your daughter experience winning and losing so she can get used to the feeling of both.

SHARE—AND YOUR FRIENDS WILL SHARE WITH YOU

We suggest; we coerce; we explain a thousand times over how other kids prefer friends who are generous. So what do we have to do to get our kids to share?

In most cases, a parent need only wait! The ability to share is a developmental milestone that does not emerge until a child has developed a sense of security about himself—and about the things he "owns."

A very young preschooler is a literal thinker. Ask him to lend you his Puffalump and he may comply, but he will be certain that his stuffed toy is gone forever. But when he reaches a maturation point somewhere between three and five years of age, he will have had enough experiences with short-term sharing to know that "Puffy" is not gone forever; his toy is merely visiting with a friend.

The ability to give and take with equanimity is an important one. For better or worse, it will affect every cooperative venture your child ever encounters. It is important, therefore, that you show your child how good (and how beneficial) sharing can be.

Don't try to force a child to share before he is ready. And don't make an older child share his prized possessions with a younger sibling. This can erode his sense of what's his. Instead, sit down with the children and separate what is yours, mine, and ours—then stick to those designations. When a child expresses an interest in his brother's or sister's toy, work out an equitable—and temporary—swap.

One of the greatest rewards of sharing, of course, is to be regarded as a potential borrower. Teach your kids to take care of their toys. That way, other kids will trust them with theirs.

WAIT YOUR TURN

Things seemed to be in relative control on the playground, until the teacher on duty heard the fourth-grade jump rope aficionados shriek. "She cut in on the line," whined one little girl, pointing to the perpetrator. "Betsy *always* cuts in on the line."

The teacher turned to Betsy for an explanation. "I didn't cut in," she insisted. "I just stopped waiting my turn."

If children have problems sharing concrete items like toys, imagine the turmoil when they try to share intangi-

118

bles—like time! Think about it. If you take my turn at jump rope, you've taken part of my playtime. If, in addition, you jump twice as long as you're supposed to, you've taken part of everybody else time. How do we exact justice—by jumping twice as long as you did? By hitting you with the rope?

Under the best of circumstances, most children are simply too antsy to wait for *anything*. They know that about one another. That's why the lines they form are virtually impenetrable. But there are some things a parent can do to help them understand that good things do eventually come to those who stand and wait.

Don't put yourself at your child's beck and call at home. Letting him wait for those things he asks for gives him a sense of appreciation for what you do—and time enough to see what goes into fulfilling his request. Ultimately, these short waits will make him a more patient person.

When a group of children is at play, an adult can reiterate the rules for anyone who is having problems playing the waiting game. Or she can give the chronic cutter something to keep her occupied while she waits. (For instance, she could suggest that Betsy count the jumps for the others rather than wait idly.)

WHEN PUSH COMES TO SHOVE

By and large, children will work out their own system of justice. Kids who "play right" will be included in a large circle of friends, while those who do not play by the rules will find themselves on the outside of the social circle looking in. Sometimes, however, children come to blows before an incident has a chance to blow over.

* * *

Two third graders, Laurie and Tricia, got into a tug-of-war over a headband that each said she found first. The teacher on duty tried to calm the girls down, but each was persistent in claiming finder's rights to the headband. Finally, Tricia pushed Laurie down and Laurie called Tricia a name, and they were sent to the principal's office.

The principal, Ms. Geiger, did not threaten the girls. Nor did she punish them. Instead, she informed them that she was giving them ''conference time'' to settle their dispute. The plan was this: Ms. Geiger would step outside her office for two minutes. When she returned, she expected each girl to tell her, briefly and truthfully, what had happened, and how she believed the situation would best be solved. Any punishment would be decided at that time.

When the allotted time was up, Ms. Geiger returned to her office and the girls told their stories. Laurie said that she saw the headband lying on the ground and pointed it out to Tricia, who immediately picked it up. Together the girls decided that since the headband was found on school property, it probably belonged to another student. Instead of continuing their squabble, they would put the headband in the Lost and Found box. No punishment was necessary.

Why do children fight? Mostly, because they are children. If they are very young or socially inexperienced, they may lack the ability to express themselves verbally. They may be legitimately angry—or totally bored. Sometimes fights erupt when children, like Laurie and Tricia, are frustrated by a situation that pulls them in two confusing directions at once (''What do I want most: this old friend or this really nice headband?'').

It may be tempting to act as referee in your child's

fights (if only to keep the blood off the carpet), but it's a temptation you should resist. We've all had our share of neighborhood battles where our child and one or two others ended the day as avowed enemies. The next morning, they head off to the bus together as if nothing had happened, leaving us to nurse our residual feelings of protectiveness and anger. Children need to learn for themselves how relationships work—even if that becomes more of a "hands on" process than you'd like.

When push comes to shove, it is imperative that your child has the tools she needs to solve her own conflicts. We like the two-minute conference—the technique we used with Laurie and Tricia—because it allows children to discuss what happened face to face. It also rewards truthfulness, ensures that all the children involved get their say, and encourages the injured parties to come to an agreement.

BULLY FOR YOU

One kid makes friends. Another makes his intimidated classmates an offer they can't refuse. The latter child is the class bully.

Making friends is an emotionally risky business. To be a friend you must open yourself up to the possibility of disappointment, hurt, and criticism. But becoming a bully takes the risk out of friendship. The bully gives nothing of himself and therefore allows for no give-and-take. In return, the bully wins nothing for himself but the appearance of friendship. It is an unsatisfying cycle that can make the aggressive child want to bully all the more.

Of course, it is very common for children to model some of their playground behavior on those macho superheroes who settle all their disputes with their fists. But those children would be quick to tell you that that posturing is only make-believe. A bully, on the other hand, is a boy or girl who may be modeling his behavior on the aggression he sees at home. His inability to express himself or to handle his problems is very real.

It's not easy to accept the news that your son has been acting out in a threatening way, or that your daughter's aggression has become a pattern, but if that news comes from your child's teacher, we hope that you will trust her enough to look for a kernel of truth. Only a teacher is in a position to see our children interact with others on a daily basis. Sure, Billy or Bobbie may seem like an angel at home, but unless we watch our children playing in groups on a regular basis, it is difficult for us to assess how successful they are at it.

Any problem your child has at school qualifies you for school-based assistance. Take advantage of it! Whether your son needs help in dealing with a specific difficulty, or your daughter simply needs to learn how to be liked, the school psychologist should be willing and able to help.

If, on the other hand, your child is *being* bullied, report the situation to the teacher. Never approach the bully himself: you may make your child a more attractive target.

GYM AND THE GENTLE ART OF ADULT INTERVENTION

It isn't easy being slow, uncoordinated, or obese in a country that is obsessed with athletics. And it isn't easy showing up for gym class knowing that yours will be the last name called when picking teams—or the first name called by the class bully. That's why kids who find it difficult to bear up during gym develop the tendency to "forget" their sneakers. They would rather accept the

122

punishment for coming to class unprepared than suffer the consequences of simply being themselves.

How we wish we could reassure parents that the drill-sergeant gym teacher they may have known simply doesn't exist! In small numbers, they do (as do overzealous teachers in *every* discipline). Still, most of the problems of physical education are not due to teacher insensitivity but to the definition and structure of the class itself. Simply put, physical education, as taught in many schools, is a system that rewards the ability to compete rather than the willingness to cooperate. At its worst, it can teach our children that physical perfection is to be prized—even over such attributes as intelligence and creativity. For those children who cannot do ten push-ups or win the relay for the team, physical education can be an education in self-consciousness or inadequacy. And that can change the way students relate to others and themselves.

A physical education teacher may see a particular child only one hour a week. He may even work at several different schools. (That's a tactic that saves the school system some money but doesn't do much for "class culture.") Still, gym class doesn't have to be a test of a child's developing ego if the physical education teacher is sensitive to his students—and to the most recent developments in his field.

As we have said, developmental learning is a method that stresses teaching to a child's strengths rather than drilling him on his academic weaknesses. It is a strategy that has revamped the way our educators approach all learning—and now, happily, it is being applied to what our children learn in gym class.

As any child who lacks the coordination to handle a ball or run fast can tell you, baseball, volleyball, relay racing, and other typical group activities are not really "team sports." After all, the most likely winner is not the team that is most cooperative but the team that is most coordinated. Whereas there is nothing wrong with a friendly game of softball or a run around the track, the well-balanced physical education curriculum should be founded upon the idea of cooperation. Problem-solving games (such as those developed by Outward Bound) get coordinated students thinking about what they can do to help their less physical peers succeed. And square dancing (a favorite among younger children) is an activity that all students can participate in equally, no matter what shape they are in.

In mathematics, a child makes a mistake on paper. Her error is visible only to her and to her teacher. But the volleyball she misses in gym can disappoint the entire team. That's where individual activities come in—to give everyone a chance to shine. Judo, archery, and even yoga are just a few of the skills teachers have used to encourage students to do their personal best. And because young students are less likely to have experienced the more "esoteric" activities (like yoga), they are experiences the students can explore as equals.

Obviously, there are limits to what educators can do to protect a vulnerable child from name-calling or bullying. Some school systems have initiated "adaptive physical education" classes, which, in addition to regularly scheduled gym classes, can help develop a child's gross motor skills, should they be lacking. Some teachers take the time to meet with parents at the beginning of the year to discuss each student's strengths and weaknesses. But every school can make its physical education program more rewarding if parents and teachers consider the gym a forum where children can try out their social *and* physical skills.

According to behavioral scientists, social intelligence is a quantifiable quality. Although you may not be able to put your finger on the personality traits that make certain children seem to stand out in a crowd, psychologists have identified the socially gifted child as one who can "read" nonverbal clues and who is at ease in social interaction.

Unfortunately, there is no such product as "instant socialization." Nor is there a magic wand a parent can wave to enhance his child's friendliness and approachability. But there is a great deal parents can do to increase a child's social IQ. For instance:

- *Let your child choose his own friends.* Kids who are allowed to decide who they want to play with are kids who feel free to develop their own personal value system. Ask them why they enjoy the company of certain friends. They'll explain in great detail that Paul, a favorite, can always be counted on to help with homework, but that Angela just might tell on you when the chips are down.

  Of course, some kids will select certain friends for shock value alone. Don't raise an eyebrow. Let them come in the front door without much notice, and they'll soon breeze out the back. A friend with a blue Mohawk might make for some short-term excitement, but long-term friendships are based on more than a hairdo.

- *Don't make your kid a target for bullies or teasers.* Maureen, the mother of a shy fourth grader, had her eyes opened when she least expected it. "In our school, each mother is expected to do playground duty once a year. And I was happy to do it—until I heard what the other kids were calling my daughter. Her real name is

125

Charlette, after my mother. But I guess she could stand to lose a few pounds because her classmates call her *Chubbette!* Can you imagine? I was just heartsick!'' Maureen buried her chin in her hands. ''Anyway, that afternoon I cried for her. But as soon as she got home we had a long talk about it—and about what I could do to help her lose the extra weight.''

Children aren't known for their tact. And parents aren't known for their clear-eyed objectivity. Heavy or thin, wearing pumped-up Air Jordan's or saddle shoes, we think our children are just beautiful. And that is how we inadvertently make them targets for the unkind comments of others.

No, clothes *don't* make the kid. And your child doesn't have to follow all the demands of fashion to fit in with the crowd. But she may need to change her self-image before she can feel a part of it all.

• *Encourage your child to bring a favorite toy to school.* A special toy can be a transitional object; that is, a security blanket (or bear, or even a Bart Simpson doll) to smooth the transition between home and school. But a popular toy can be an icebreaker, too, since it provides a focal point for kids to gather and play around.

Just be sure to check with your child's teacher before allowing her to bring her favorite New Kids action figure to school. Some teachers don't allow any toys in the classroom. If you do get the go-ahead, make sure your child's playthings are clearly labeled. Nothing turns buddies into battlers like a property dispute.

• *Sensitize your children to the uniqueness of others.* Among seven-year-old Allen's neighbors are the residents of a group home for people with cerebral palsy. Allen, who had seen the residents on their afternoon walks, never asked his mother what cerebral palsy was. He simply kept his distance.

Last Halloween, however, his mother made the group home a special stop while trick-or-treating with Allen and his sister. "Allen was afraid," she reported. "At first he refused to go in. But when he saw how warmly the residents greeted us—and the candy in their hands—he followed his sister inside.

"On the way home, he asked me about cerebral palsy—what it's like to have it, and how people get it. I assured him that it wasn't something he could catch, like the flu. Now when he sees the residents outside, he's still a little standoffish, but he always says hello."

And isn't that how all friendships begin—by conquering our fear and simply saying hello?

- *Encourage your child to make friends of all ages.* Many of our school-age children live in an age-segregated society. They spend all day in the company of their peers. They go home to neighborhoods populated by families of roughly the same age. Their grandparents may live hundreds of miles away—or in one of those adult communities that do not welcome children. These kids may be suffering from experienced citizen deprivation!

Each of your older neighbors and friends is a vast repository of local history, personal knowledge, and hands-on skills. Putting your children in their care is like delivering them to a living library.

You may want to remind your children to treat their older friends with respect. You may even decide to chaperone their first few visits. But the age barrier is one limit you'll want your child to break.

- *Finally, leave those kids alone*! Let your child make

friends at her own pace. Don't force her to warm up before she's ready, or handpick "more suitable" chums than she is choosing for herself. And don't involve yourself in any childhood tiffs.

Learning to play is every bit as important as learning to read or write. And like most hands-on learning processes, it works best when well-intentioned adults keep their hands *off*.

7
Making the Grade

There is a certain way some parents have of coming to grips with a less-than-positive school report. They wring it in their hands as though they want to choke it.

Being surprised with bad news from school is right up there with going for what you think will be a routine dental exam, only to discover that you are in dire need of root canal work. The only difference is that no parent really ought to be surprised by news from school, whether that news is good or bad. If you are a member of the Parent-Teachers Organization—and you should be— then you will be in the know about school policies (like the timing of progress reports). And if you consider yourself a partner in your child's education, you will have already touched base with your child's teacher.

But many parents are still squeamish about "bothering'' the teacher. And some will never attend a PTC meeting that isn't mandatory. Even in these cases, there are a great many ways to tell whether school is bringing out the best in a child, whether grades accurately reflec progress, and whether it is the child or the curriculum that is "weak in math." Best of all, this information is available not just by special request. Your child delivers it to your doorstep every day—some days more willingly than others.

HOW TO CHECK TESTS, OR X MARKS THE SPOT

"Oh no, the bus is here! Quick—sign my spelling test, okay, Dad?''

Every parent has signed on the fly. And there's really no harm in giving that quiz or homework assignment a cursory check *once in a while*. But if test and homework signing has a tendency to slip your child's mind, you'd better grab him before he slips out the door!

Weekly quizzes may be multiple-choice quickies; they may add up to only a miniscule percentage of your child's total grade, but testing is an important measure of progress for both a teacher and student. And it's a smart parent who uses weekly test results to keep an eye on both.

Teaching, like parenting, can be a humbling experience. A teacher may feel that she just taught the best long division of her career, only to find out after testing the material that she lost her class somewhere between the dividend and the divisor. A good teacher, then, will look on testing as a trail marker along the way to learning. It lets her know if her chosen route of instruction is getting her class where they want to go. It also lets her know precisely where any stragglers have gotten lost.

Beware, however, the teacher who is quick to fail small children, especially if she seems determined to make that

F count! Kindergarteners and first and second graders are faced with a learning challenge greater than that faced by many college students. They are exposed to vast amounts of basic material in a short time, and, because that material forms the foundation of all future learning, it is crucial that they master it. Allowing a young student to fail smothers the joy of learning. A teacher who fails our youngest students is a teacher who fails to understand the purpose of testing. Small children cannot be held responsible for what they have not been properly taught.

A test doesn't have to be a four-letter word if it is handled properly. At their best, regular quizzes can be an early warning system, alerting you to any areas your child simply doesn't "get." Tests can help a student organize her thoughts. They can even give a child the chance to experience pressure in carefully measured doses, thereby increasing his resilience as a person. Or they can simply give a student a chance to succeed.

When checking a youngster's tests, bear in mind that his grade is not the most important piece of information on the paper. An *A* may be a welcome sight, but when it comes to educational troubleshooting, *X* really does mark the spot. Focus on those questions your child answered wrong. Are there any similarities between them? Do you notice any patterns between these incorrect answers and those on previous tests? Wrong answers aren't failures. They are clues that can lead you to areas in which your child may need extra help.

You certainly don't want your child to fail a test, nor do you want the test to fail your child. If your son consistently performs well in class but tests below par, he simply may not do well with paper-and-pencil tasks. Speak to his teacher. If his instruction is multisensory, perhaps his tests should be, too.

Quizzes and tests are not the be-all-and-end-all when

it comes to determining whether a child is making the grade. Certainly, as much practical "data" about how your son or daughter may be adjusting can be gleaned from the doodles in his or her notebook margins as from any more formal yardstick. Still, a child cannot be expected to diagnose her own learning or social problems. And that is why it is important for you to examine your child's attitude toward learning—even if your patience is tested in the process.

HOMEWORK 101—A CRASH COURSE FOR PARENTS

It is 6:00 P.M. in the Mara household. So far, George Mara has loosened his tie and stowed his briefcase in the corner. He is at the stove, stirring a boiling pot of pasta. Meanwhile, his wife, Diane, is doing a slow boil herself. It is her turn to help their daughter, Nora, with her homework. Next to that, cooking—even after a long day at work—is a snap.

"For Pete's sake, Nora—creative-writing assignments are supposed to be fun! Now *here* . . ." Diane slaps a freshly sharpened pencil on the table. "Be creative—and *have fun*."

Nora pushes the pencil aside. "I don't know, Mom. I don't think I got the assignment right. I can never read Ms. Mursky's assignments. She has terrible handwriting."

Diane had seen this ploy before. "But Nora, we talked to Ms. Mursky about that problem, remember? She promised you she'd print."

Nora buries her face in her hands. Finally, she whines, "So maybe she forgot."

Across the room, George has reached his boiling point. "And I guess you forgot what I told you about turning

132

thirty minutes of homework into a three-hour battle. We're tired, we're angry, and we've had it, Nora.''

"But Dad, I—''

George waved her away. "Go to your room, Nora. We'll talk about this after dinner.''

With that, Nora goes off to her room where she spends a few minutes coloring an apology picture for her parents. She knows that her parents will feel better after they've eaten. She also knows that after dinner she will be too tired to write her story, so her mother will help her.

Nora will have escaped homework for the second time this week.

Nora and the many children like her have learned their lessons well—and what they have learned can't be found in any book. Nora is only in the third grade. But she has already mastered the fact that she can get more attention by balking at her books than she can by quietly completing her assignments. She has also learned that all she needs to do to get her homework done for her is push her mother's guilt button.

In many ways, bringing a child who has put in five hours at school together with a parent who has put in a long, hard day is like bringing a lighted match to a gas can. Something is bound to blow. But that doesn't make it okay to fight over homework or to turn what should be a fifteen-minute assignment into a three-hour marathon.

No kid should be bringing home a schoolbag full of angst. We want our children to be intellectually challenged, not overwhelmed. But the way a child approaches homework doesn't only reveal the way he relates to learning. It reveals the way he relates to you. If your son complains that he finds it difficult to concentrate at home, he may simply be over-stimulated—or he may be confused by the family dynamics. If he routinely stretches assignments (and your nerves) beyond the snapping point, he may be telling you that he resents spending his off-duty hours working on his weakest subjects. Or he may be waiting for you to become frustrated enough to do it for him.

Despite evidence to the contrary, the purpose of homework is not to drive parents off the deep end. A take-home assignment reinforces what a child learns during the day studies. It allows a student to work at greater length and depth on projects and studies he finds especially interesting. Homework can teach a child to accept responsibility for his work, his grades, and his behavior. And, because even the smallest assignments reflect a child's strengths and weaknesses, a teacher can fit them together like a puzzle, painting a more vivid picture of a student's learning style, preferences, and potential difficulties.

A HAND OFF—HANDS ON DILEMMA
Offer no help with homework, and your child can flounder. Help too much, and the picture is distorted. The following suggestions can prevent a well-meaning parent from becoming a homework hindrance.

- *Be sure your child understands the assignment*. Ask her to read it aloud, then explain it back to you in her own words.

- *Be available during homework time*. Physically, you may be within arm's reach, but if you are cooking or busy with chores, you may seem a thousand miles away to your child. Be there for him, mentally and physically. Otherwise, he may feel that he's disturbing you.

- *Find the right time for homework.* Ideally, assignments should be begun when the child is neither too wired nor too tired.

- *Eliminate distractions.* Unplug the phone. Turn off the TV and the radio. Then listen. If your household is still noisy, you may have to quiet those boisterous teenagers or silence the family squabbles that *you* stopped hearing.

- *Keep your biases and phobias to yourself.* Parents have a tendency to pass these down like dominant genes. Don't accept a child's failure in a subject just because it is a class you failed, too. And don't say things like "I was never much good at math, either." You will just encourage your child not to try.

- *Be consistent.* The way *you* divide fractions may be quicker, but the teacher is using her method for a reason. Stick to it—*without shortcuts.*

- *Check homework without correcting it.* Unless you allow your child's teacher to see his mistakes, she cannot get an accurate picture of his progress—or lack of it. You're not just cheating the teacher, you're cheating your own child.

- *Ask your child's teacher how long he believes homework assignments should take.* Ideally, your school's homework policy should be spelled out as part of its philosophy. (A commonly used rule of thumb is that children should receive about ten minutes of homework for each grade: first graders, ten minutes; second graders, twenty minutes, etc.) If your child seems to be taking an inordinately long time on an assignment, check with the teacher. Your child may simply be a slow worker. But if he or she consistently gets half of the questions wrong, it is time for a parent-teacher conference.

- *Provide your child with a homework book*. Any child whose favorite refrain is "but we didn't *have* any" can be made more responsible for his assignments if his parents and teacher give him a "homework book." This book can be any kind of a spiral-bound notebook in which the child writes his daily assignments. After he has copied the assignment from the blackboard, the teacher reads what he has copied. If the assignment is correct, she signs and dates the page and sends him home. When the child has completed his homework, he shows it to his parents. If the assignment was completed, they sign and date the book. Last but not least, the child himself signs the book and returns it to school. It may seem that the homework book goes through more signings than the Declaration of Independence, but such a procedure does help a child to assume responsibility for his work. In fact, we encourage parents and teachers to schedule a meeting two weeks after the homework book is introduced. By that time, many students no longer need a reminder.

- *If your child rejects your help, leave him alone*. Independence is the most important lesson a child can learn! It may not be easy for you to back off, but consider it your contribution to his developing sense of self.

REPORT CARDS

Karen was getting impatient. It had been several minutes since she handed her seven-year-old daughter's report card to her husband, Mike.

"Well, what do you think?" she prompted.

Mike stared at the card, then shook his head slowly.

"I think I'll have to go back to second grade. I need to learn how to read this thing!"

No doubt about it—grades just aren't what they used to be. In most public schools, it is no longer common practice to reduce several months of a child's work to a simple grade of A through F. And number grades have become an endangered species.

Like Mike, you may be taken aback by the newer grading systems. You may even feel that they are unnecessarily complicated, or that there is nothing so precise and understandable as a letter or number grade. But nothing could be further from the truth. Schools are no longer stratified into clearly differentiated class levels. Teachers across the United States have stopped teaching to "maturational norms" and begun to instruct each child based on her own individual strengths and weaknesses. Is it fair, then, to rate a child's performance by basing it on a maturational norm? Doesn't it make sense to use checklists, like the one that follows, to remark upon all her strengths and weaknesses, including her attitude, her ability to concentrate, and the quality of her effort?

Report cards today may bear little resemblance to those you got as a child. Some school systems even grade developmentally. Your child's social studies grade, for instance, may be a *4B*, meaning that—in this subject—your third grader is working at the level of a *B* student in fourth grade. But no matter how your child's experience is being graded, her report card is still one of the most reliable gauges of academic performance available to a parent. That's because your child's report card is a distillation of *all* her work: in class and out; tests and projects; from her class participation to an assessment of her motivation.

	Usually	Sometimes	Never
Academic Behaviors			
Pays attention to teacher	_____	_____	_____
Is able to sit at desk	_____	_____	_____
Begins work on time	_____	_____	_____
Can attend to task	_____	_____	_____
Completes assigned work	_____	_____	_____
Social Behaviors			
Obeys class rules	_____	_____	_____
Gets along with peers	_____	_____	_____
Respects authority	_____	_____	_____
Can share and wait turn	_____	_____	_____
Subject Areas			
Reading			
Recognizes letters	_____	_____	_____
Recognizes words	_____	_____	_____
Reads with understanding	_____	_____	_____

*This is a partial listing only

Just the thought that our child may lack the motivation to give school her best shot can drive us to distraction. We think of the competitive world she will enter and wonder whether she will be caught unprepared. We push her into "enriching experiences," hoping an idea will catch fire.

The good news is that most kids will become motivated on their own when we allow them the freedom to learn independently—somewhere between the third and fifth grades. But high motivation doesn't necessarily translate into high grades. Students may be especially bright in one class but average-achievers in another. That doesn't mean that they aren't working to potential.

There are thousands of children in our schools who, at age six or nine, feel that they are already disappointments to their families. Many of them are children who have been told, simply, to do their best. But when their best earns them only average grades, they begin to think that their best isn't good enough. These children come to school with their stomachs in knots—and their egos in a twist.

Learn to accept your children the way they accept you: imperfections and all. And don't reward As with money, gifts, or privileges. Your child may find it easy to get As in those subjects that come naturally. What is more deserving of a reward: an easy A or a hard-earned B?

There is nothing less motivating than a class we don't understand. If you believe that there is a gap between your child's potential and his motivation, don't lecture. Don't bargain. In fact, don't do anything until you're sure that your son or daughter doesn't need extra help. Ask your child's teacher to double-check his knowledge of both the theory behind the problem and the process needed to arrive at a correct answer. Then keep an eye on his tests and quizzes to check his progress.

You may also consider your child's standardized test scores when determining his potential, but beware: standardized tests are given to a class as a group. No allowance is made for personal learning styles, a child's physical coordination (which may affect how accurately he fills in the dots), or even how he feels that day.

Testing is a tool, not an end in itself. Use test data not as an indicator of how a child measures up to his peers but as a baseline on which to chart his progress. If his scores are up or on a par with the year before, he has connected with his school and its curriculum. If they have declined, it is time to intervene. Set up a meeting as soon as possible with his teacher, principal, and perhaps his counselor.

Finally, your child's demeanor should tell you more about his motivation than his test scores and grades put together. An interested, enthusiastic child who charges onto the bus every morning is likely to be charged up about school too. But if a student's attitude is negative, the prognosis may be quite the opposite.

RETENTION: THE GIFT OF TIME OR THEFT OF A YEAR?

"I can't say I didn't see it coming," admitted Marcia, the mother of a seven-year-old who will be repeating the first grade this year. "At first, Stephen was thrilled to be in 'big' school. He loved his teacher. But he couldn't focus on anything for more than a few seconds. By Christmas he was going for extra help with his letter sounds. By Easter he was completely befuddled by reading. So when his teacher suggested that we get together in May, I had my suspicions about what she was going to suggest. But it still hit me like a ton of bricks."

Our hopes for our children are built on many things: love, competition, even resentment for those activities we may have tried and failed. As parents, we tend to pile these hopes one atop the other, like blocks, never thinking that we need something to hold them in place other than our own determination. That is why, when reality gives our dreams a bump, it all comes down on us like a ton of bricks, the way it did on Marcia.

Of all the decisions a parent must make throughout a child's lifetime, keeping a child back is among the most difficult. In many ways, it is an experience that goes head-to-head against everything you know about being a good parent. You may have been quick to come to your young son's assistance, but now you must watch him struggle and fail. You may have been a warm and loving parent to your daughter, but now you are feeling frustrated, angry, and disappointed with her progress.

And if you are the type of parent who looks to current research or professional thought to shed light on such issues, you are not likely to be comforted by the findings. Retention has been discredited in more than sixty research studies. In fact, one recent study indicates that 40 percent of the students kept back retained less knowledge and scored lower on standardized tests than they did the year before. Moreover, in those studies that matched a group of students who were held back with a similar (developmentally below grade level) group who were promoted, the held-back group lagged even farther behind after repeating the grade. In addition, the children who were retained were found to have fewer friends and to suffer from lower self-esteem. In the long run, they were even more likely to have attendance problems and, ultimately, to drop out of school altogether.

Certainly, some children who leave kindergarten or first grade labeled "below grade level" *are* promoted. Many of these children will outgrow their immaturity and catch up to the rest of the class, though often not until the end of second or beginning of third grade.

Retention doesn't have to be the end of the world. It may be preferable to promotion when a child is the "slow one" in a rapidly progressing class, a state of affairs that can also take its toll on the child's self-esteem. Retention can be a new beginning: a fresh start, tempered by an additional year of maturity.

As most practitioners will agree, retention is least likely to cause adverse effects if it is introduced early in a child's educational history—before she has become wedded to a peer group. And there is little evidence that retaining your child will damage him emotionally if your entire family approaches it positively. Still, it would be wise to investigate carefully the teacher's reasons for retention. Even the most positive parent cannot accept the gift of time with anything but suspicion if she remains conflicted about it in her heart.

Is your child failing across the board? If she is weaker in one or two subjects than others, perhaps she would benefit more from extra help than she would by staying back. Is she wedded to her peer group? If so, the emotional detriment of staying back must be weighed against any academic benefit. Is the teacher accepting a wide developmental range as "normal"? Or is she simply weeding out those students who need more help and therefore take more time? Is your child going from one type of learning experience (i.e., developmental) to another (perhaps more traditional)? If so, it may be a form of academic culture shock, rather than the curriculum, that is confusing her.

If the teacher answers all your questions to your satisfaction, and you agree that your child would benefit from being retained, it is time for you to take control. First, you must tell your child that he is being retained (and please don't call it "staying back") so that he will have more time to learn and grow. Emphasize that you and his teacher care for him and that you know this "gift of time" will help him to feel better and do better in school. Don't be surprised if your child is more ready to accept the idea of retention than you were. Kids know when they aren't making it academically.

After speaking with the child, you must tell all relatives, friends, and neighbors who may interact with your son or daughter that the decision has been made—and that you, as parents, know it is the correct one. Never let well-meaning friends or relatives undermine your decision. And if necessary, correct anyone who makes your child feel "bad" or "stupid" because he has been retained. Let them know, under no uncertain circumstances, that you view this as a positive step, one that will allow your child to be and do his best.

If, on the other hand, you disagree with the idea of retention, it is your right and responsibility as a parent to dispute it.

Begin by requesting a copy of the school's promotion/retention policy to see which criteria were used to make the decision. Be wary of a school that cannot produce a copy of its retention policy in writing. The school may be whittling down the class so it fits the curriculum, when it should be approaching education from the other way around.

Review your child's school records (yes, you have a right to see them!), standardized test scores, and report cards. Then make an objective list of his strengths and weaknesses. Do they really fit the retention policy? Is it possible that your child has a learning disability? Are there any extenuating circumstances, such as illnesses, family problems, ongoing parent-teacher conflicts, or stressful changes that may have affected your child's performance? (Remember, even those changes you consider fortunate—such as your remarriage or new job—can be stressful to your child.) If so, add these to your notes.

Make an appointment to meet with all the school personnel who are directly involved with your child's education, including his teacher, the school principal, and his counselor. Report your findings. Then share all the information you have discovered with them, including any research results that may be coloring your perspective.

You may be the most respectful parent to ever cross the school threshold, but what you know can make some educators defensive. They may try to put you on the spot by asking you to make specific recommendations about alternative approaches to retention. Be prepared! Your child might benefit from any number of options, including promotion with remedial instruction, summer school, a special education evaluation, professional tutoring, a reading or math ''buddy,'' or a developmentally oriented, multisensory approach, allowing students with varied skill levels and abilities to work together toward a common goal. If all else fails, you may simply ask that the final decision be delayed until the child has had a chance to improve his grades.

The point of this chapter is that you don't have to let your kid bottom out before you get to the bottom of his problems. Education is a continuous process. By being a constant, interested partner in your child's education, you will always stay in the know about your child's progress.

8
Does Experience Make the Best Teacher?

Roberta Kelly, second grade teacher, hears her first bell of the day at 5:30 A.M.; that's when she gets up to shower, dress, and make lunches for her own children, all of whom must be at school by 7:45.

By 7:10, the children have already eaten breakfast. Now they are arguing over who gets the toy surprise from the cereal box. Checking to see that their faces are clean, Roberta wraps the kids in their bulky coats, hands them each a lunch box, and passes them into the care of their father, who must be at work by 8:00.

By the time she arrives at school, Ms. Kelly has already mapped out, in her mind, what she must do to prepare for the day. First she must organize her teaching materials: that means photocopying worksheets, writing the characteristics of the mammal on the blackboard, and gathering all the material she will need to explain to twenty-five seven-year-olds why a dolphin is not really a fish.

But there is a fly (decidedly *not* a mammal) in the ointment. One of her students, Jack, is having learning problems. Before school is the only time this week that the members of the school evaluation team can meet with Ms. Kelly and Jack's parents to discuss Jack's problem and decide whether some in-depth testing is needed. After asking an office volunteer to help out with the photocopying, she rushes off to the meeting.

When the bell rings, her second graders enter the classroom, fully expecting to be challenged, entertained, helped—and liked by their teacher. Meanwhile, there are a number of ongoing situations that Ms. Kelly finds it difficult to like. Susan is complaining that she doesn't feel well. Her teacher wonders if Susan is suffering from an attack of conscience: Susan has a science project due today, but she doesn't seem to have one at her desk. While Thomas announces that he has forgotten his lunch (for the second time this week), and the rest of the class protect their science projects from each other, Ms. Kelly takes attendance and begins the lesson.

Reading is scheduled first, when the children are most alert. The aide she was counting on will be absent today, so Ms. Kelly must juggle to provide a challenging environment for one reading group while playing catch-up with another. Not that it matters. Less than a half-hour into the lesson, an assembly is called to welcome several visiting foreign students to the school. While they perform a song in their native tongue, Ms. Kelly plans the rest of the day. After the program, her class will go to gym. The teacher has learned from experience that her students will come back to class either like zoned-out zombies or hyped-up hysterics.

Ms. Kelly has cafeteria duty today, so she'll have only fifteen of the contracted thirty minutes she usually has for lunch. In fact, she'll barely have time to call a student's mother to find out why her daughter came to school crying that morning.

The afternoon is more of the same. "Played-out" from recess, the second graders seem ready for nap time, not social studies. But Ms. Kelly is not to be outdone. She provides storytime, math games, or visits to learning and listening centers where students can work alone or in small groups to reinforce what they have learned. At 2:00 P.M., Officer Bob comes in with McGruff the Crime Dog to talk about drugs. Ms. Kelly barely has time to scrawl the assignment on the board before the final bell rings and the children are escorted to their buses.

At last, Roberta Kelly can catch her breath. "Showtime" is over. She doesn't have to be "on" anymore. But that doesn't mean her day is over. There are papers to correct, phone calls to make, lessons to be reviewed for the next day, and notes to be written to two parents. She needs to make practice phonics sheets and run off copies on the duplicating machine. (The school aide is supposed to do this, but she needs two days notice. She assists twelve teachers.)

Gathering up her belongings, Ms. Kelly wonders whether the creative alternatives she devised for her advanced readers really kept them challenged, whether Melissa was able to stay on task better today than yesterday, and whether Richie has a bladder control problem or is avoiding work that is too hard for him by making frequent trips to the bathroom.

She leaves the building at 4:45, nearly twelve hours after her day began.

Who among us hasn't collapsed after a child's birthday party when fifteen seven-year-olds spent four hours wreaking havoc on cake, balloons, and our nerves? And who hasn't ever whispered "better you than me!" when dropping a rowdy, rambunctious child off at school—and into his unsuspecting teacher's care?

As Roberta Kelly's "typical" day illustrates, teaching is an unparalleled professional challenge with immeasurable rewards. It is a daily test of a professional's skill and knowledge. It tries one's versatility, requiring its practitioners to dry a child's tears one minute and whet her appetite for learning the next. But most of all, teaching is the ultimate test of endurance, the only known job in which one is expected to have the patience of Job, the judgment of Solomon, and, some would say, a certain desire for martyrdom in order to survive, if not succeed.

Our early teachers may have been saints or devils. They may have been underpaid and unappreciated. But they will never go unremembered. Whether she did it with round-edged scissors or a painfully sharp tongue, one of our first teachers trimmed away the last vestiges of our babyhood and pointed the way to independent learning. And whether she was "good" or "bad" by our sophisticated adult standards, one of these teachers helped us form—out of construction paper and glue—an appreciation for formal education. It is that appreciation that leads us now as we search for the best educational experiences for our children.

Does experience make the best teacher? It depends on the experience—and the teacher. As you'll see, there is a great deal you can do to make your teacher's experience as satisfying for her as it is for your child.

As to what makes the best teacher, we'll just say this: you are about as likely to find the "perfect" teacher as you are to be the perfect parent. Your child's teacher may not be your ideal, but teachers, in general, are getting better every day.

Karen and her sister, Kathy, were one year apart in school. As in many families, the girls played certain roles within the household. Kathy, it had been decided, was the "sweet sister": an average student but generous and kind to a fault. Karen, meanwhile, tore up the academic turf. She passed classes without cracking a book and hurtled over the difficult test questions that stopped lesser students cold. When the time came, Karen was accepted to several top-ranked colleges. But in the end, she decided to stay near her sister who had enrolled at the state university as a humanities major.

When Kathy graduated with a *B* average, she enrolled in the university's teacher's certification program. But as Karen's graduation approached, it became clear that although the girls had attended the same school, their family had very different expectations of them.

"When Karen and I came home over spring break, the hot topic of conversation seemed to be what each of us was planning to 'do' with our educations. Obviously, I was going to be a teacher," said Kathy. "And that was okay with everybody. But when Karen announced that she was looking into certification, too, all hell broke loose. Teaching elementary school was fine for me, but Karen was a *good* student—and a math major, to boot. Couldn't she get a *real* job for *real* money somewhere in business?"

In the early part of the twentieth century (when our parents' attitudes were forming), teaching was considered a safe, secure career. And because it centered on the nurturing of children, teaching became a popular metier for women, even at a time when it wasn't popular for women to work. But allowing women the "freedom" to teach (especially single women who had no husbands to discipline them) was often simply another way to keep women under control. In fact, choosing to become a teacher in the "roaring" 1920s meant choosing a life-style that was very much like that of a nun.

TYPICAL TEACHER'S CONTRACT FOR WOMEN IN 1920

Miss _____ agrees:

1. Not to get married

2. Not to keep the company of men

3. Not to loiter in ice cream stores

4. Not to smoke cigarettes

5. Not to drink beer, wine, or whiskey

6. Not to dress in bright colors

7. Not to dye her hair

8. To wear at least two petticoats

9. Not to use face powder, mascara, or paint the lips

A teacher who doesn't smoke cigarettes or drink whiskey today is a teacher who is concerned about her health—not her image. Moreover, teaching has attracted more than a few "good men"—and it would be unthinkable that they be subjected to such stringent rules of propriety. To that extent, the perception of teaching has changed. But like nursing (and even parenting), teaching is a profession traditionally associated with women. Although it is no longer strictly "women's work," teaching remains underpaid and undervalued as a career. The rules written in the 1920s may not apply today, but as long as we continue to discourage students like Karen or suggest that "those who can, do; and those who can't, teach," our heritage of sexism will live on.

That said, it is no wonder that our veteran teachers feel taken for granted, taken advantage of, or just taken. Nor can we seriously question their motives when we hear that the number of public school teachers decreases every year or that our most gifted young adults are choosing to share those gifts in more lucrative professions.

Still, there is good news on the horizon. Though our nation's schools are still operating under a teacher shortage—parciularly a lack of academically talented teachers, minority teachers, and instructors in the areas of math and science—more and better qualified students *are* choosing teaching as a profession. According to the National Center for Education Statistics, the annual number of new teachers rose 20 percent from 1984 to 1986, and the upward trend seems to be continuing.

Not only that, but your child is more likely than ever to be taught by an academically gifted teacher. In the last five years, forty-six states have instituted or are developing tests students must pass in order to qualify for teacher certification. At least twenty-seven states require that students meet a minimum grade-point average or standardized test score before they can be admitted to teacher education. And in a sweeping move to encourage excellence among experienced teachers, the National Board for Professional Teaching Standards has announced that it has hired a research team to design what will ultimately be a series of tests to identify the best teachers in various fields. The aim of the project, according to the board, is to pinpoint a distinguished group of board-certified professionals who will enhance the status of teaching, raise salaries, and, by their example, attract more talented people into the field.

The trend toward hiring more knowledgable teachers has already begun. Because schools are increasingly selecting those teaching candidates who majored in subjects other than education, your child is more likely to learn about the Hanging Gardens of Babylon from someone who majored in history. And because teacher education students in 1988 typically maintained a *B* average or better in college and scored slightly above the national average on the SATs, today's teachers don't have to adopt a "do-as-I-say" attitude about learning. Their do-as-I-do study habits make them an example that any student would be well advised to follow.

BUT WHO IS YOUR CHILD'S TEACHER, REALLY?

"If the statistics are encouraging, that's great," said one far-from-convinced mother. "But knowing that better teachers are in the pipeline doesn't help me this year. Do you know what the kids call my son's teacher? Middle-aged Mutant Ninja Teacher. And you know what? They're being kind."

WHEN BAD THINGS HAPPEN TO GOOD TEACHERS

You don't have to be a media expert to know that the image of teaching and teachers has taken a real battering. It was nearly thirty years ago that we, as a nation, responded to a book called *Why Johnny Can't Read* by collectively pointing the finger at Johnny's teacher. Three decades and innumerable research grants later, we have learned a great deal about the critical role that parents play in directing and maintaining the quality of a child's education. We have discovered that an interested, involved parent can make the difference between watching

Johnny come marching home with a book under his arm or a video game cassette.

But if the case for parental involvement has been made, why are we still reading headlines like "How Teachers Are Failing Our Children"? Why does the story about the teenager who graduated from high school unable to read his diploma get more airplay than the stories of the thousands of kids who graduate each year, go on to college, or pursue worthwhile careers? Why are teachers still getting none of the praise and all of the blame?

"So who's supposed to get the blame for the thousands of kids who are undereducated at a time when taxes have never been higher?" one father sputtered. "I can't be in school all day to make sure that my child is 'being challenged.' I'm a businessman. Maybe if the school principal ran the school more like a business and expected teachers to do what they're being paid to do, Johnny would be able to read. What's more, he'd be reading something other than his unemployment check."

More than ever, Americans are feeling ripped off. And in many communities, they're *getting* ripped off. While local taxes hit the stratosphere, services have hit rock bottom. Teachers may complain that they aren't getting enough respect, but they're getting a great deal more than many members of the community they serve. As some parents see it, teachers get twelve months pay for nine months work. If they are tenured, they are not subject to the layoffs now plaguing the parents of the students they teach. And whether their performance is good, bad, or merely mediocre, the union will protect their right to earn a living.

While the typical American family tightens its belt, the local teachers are asking for a cost-of-living raise.

Have committed teachers gone the way of the one-room schoolhouse? Do they really believe that dedication is something that money can buy? What do teachers really want, anyway?

WHAT DO TEACHERS WANT?

"Merit pay? Semester-long sabbaticals? Are you kidding?" laughed one elementary school veteran. "I'd be happy if I just got twenty-two kids who were well rested, well fed, and ready to learn every day!"

Parental consciousness about education beginning at home has never been higher. Still, some parents simply aren't doing all they can to become active partners in the educational process. They send their children to school unprepared for the day. They use the playground as their personal day-care center, dropping their children off hours before the start of school. Often, the same parents are the first in line to tell the principal that they hold the teacher completely responsible for the fact that "little Dave or Diana just isn't taking to school."

No matter how the media distort the truth, there are hundreds of Mr. Chips and Miss Doves hard at work in the public schools. But there isn't a teacher alive who won't do a better job when parents begin to do theirs.

What do teachers want? Ask! You'd be surprised at how little it takes to make them happy. A few scraps of felt to make a feltboard; a flag from another country for geography day; a parent who has the time (and the camera) to videotape a class dramatic production—these are the things at the top of teachers' wish lists. If you're feeling ambitious, you can type the list up and circulate it at the PTO. If not, give what you can, whether it be time, materials, or money.

Most of all, teachers want to feel that they are not alone in the educational process. Instead of running to the principal with a laundry list of complaints, go to the school board meeting and lobby for increased teacher input at the upper levels of educational decision making. Maybe if those who teach the texts had more to say about their content, little Dave and Diana would find their classes more interesting.

Obviously, good morale isn't something a teacher can eat (though it is bound to leave a good taste in her mouth). Teachers do understand that money can't buy happiness in any profession, but pay remains a difficult issue. So do on-the-job bugaboos like increasing paperwork, restricted mobility, and school system dysfunction. But these are all problems that can be worked out when parents truly become accountable to teachers, and teachers become more accountable to their students.

As to the difficulties of dealing with a "Middle-aged Mutant Ninja Teacher" (or discovering which came first: your child's bad behavior or his teacher's bad attitude), those are best handled face-to-face, during the parent-teacher conference.

THE PARENT-TEACHER CONFERENCE

We are always amazed at the number of parents who meet with a teacher only in case of an academic emergency. Odder, still, are those parents who would never think of dropping their child into the lap of a strange babysitter but who will gladly drop that same child off on the first day of school without so much as a glance at the teacher who will be caring for him for the next nine months.

Parents are a bit like Pavlov's dog. If they hear a teacher's voice only during times of stress and strain, they will come to associate that teacher with negative situations. At the sound of the school bell, they may even find themselves becoming defensive, accusative, or uncommunicative. It is ideal, therefore, for a parent to make contact with his child's teacher at the beginning of the year before an academic emergency has had a chance to arise. This will give the parent a chance to establish a rapport while both parties are at their best.

After that, a parent-teacher conference can take place anytime either party feels it is warranted: after report cards are issued, when a child seems to be struggling, when his at-home concerns affect his in-school performance, when he seems unhappy with or frightened by his teacher, or when his behavior takes an uncharacteristic turn.

TWO HEADS ARE BETTER THAN ONE

"Her brother was a holy terror," admitted Tina, the mother of a third and first grader, "but little Teresa was always the shy, quiet type. Or at least I *thought* she was, until she came home with that note from her teacher saying that Teresa had bitten two classmates during recess. Needless to say, I was beside myself. That very afternoon, I left Teresa and Michael with their grandmother and went straight to the school to find out what had happened.

"But when I got there, the office secretary said that Teresa's teacher wouldn't see me without an appointment! I slammed the note down on the counter. How could I discipline Teresa? Until I talked to the teacher, I didn't really know what had happened. And if she didn't want to see me that day, why did she send me that upsetting note?"

That it takes four arms to control a toddler is an old joke among parents. That it takes two sets of eyes to clearly see the personality and potential of a school-age child is the time-honored truth.

A parent sees with eyes of love, and he sees only what goes on at home. A teacher, on the other hand, has an opportunity to observe a child more objectively, both as an individual and as a part of his peer group. Only when parent and teacher get together, then, can either of them get the whole picture. But not if the parent arrives at the conference an emotional wreck, as Tina did—and not if she catches the teacher unprepared.

Chances are, Teresa's teacher understood Tina's concern. When a child's behavior seems out of character, it is as if she is waving a red flag. Any parent who views it as a cry for help will naturally run to her child's aid. But the problem that seems so immediate and crucial to you may not seem so to a veteran teacher. For all Tina knows, there may be two other biters in her daughter's class, and Teresa may simply be following suit. Still, popping in on a teacher is no way to find that out. A surprise visit from you can put a teacher on the defensive—and because the teacher will not have had time to pull her records together, it may net you a whole lot less information.

Treat the teacher as you would any other professional. Unless she has asked you to do so, don't call her at home. And never show up unexpectedly. Instead, make an appointment to meet at a mutually agreeable time. If you really want to get on a teacher's good side, try to schedule your visit during "office hours" as you would when meeting with your lawyer or doctor. If that's impossible, ask to see her before the school day begins or in the afternoon before she leaves the building.

Most of all, arrive prepared. Because each parent and teacher views a child from his own unique vantage point, they can be natural allies. But a parent and teacher together can paint an accurate picture of a child's academic situation only if each adds some of the detail.

If your child is exhibiting peculiar behaviors, as Teresa was, you will want to discuss those behaviors with your child. Talk to her about what brought the specific outburst on, then find out how she feels about school in general. Encourage her to discuss all her likes and dislikes about the teacher, her classmates, or the curriculum.

If you will be meeting with the teacher to discuss academic concerns, you will want to review your child's report card, progress reports, tests, quizzes, homework papers, and any other materials your child brings home from school. But don't automatically accept low grades as proof that your child is "not trying" or "not working to potential." These papers provide valuable evidence of your child's natural talents—and those inclinations can be key factors in motivating a struggling student.

Finally, make a list of questions you wish to ask your child's teacher. Conversations do wander—and you may find yourself wandering off toward home without ever having asked the questions that brought you to the meeting!

The National Committee for Citizens in Education suggests that these questions form the basis of the parent-teacher conference.

- Is my child performing at grade level in basic skills?
- Does my child have strengths and weaknesses in major subject areas?
- Does my child need help in any academic subject? In social adjustment?
- If so, what help and special services are available?
- Has my child regularly completed the classwork and homework assigned?

- Has my child attended class regularly?
- Does my child get along well with classmates?
- Does my child participate in class?
- How are his or her work habits and attitude?
- How do you (the teacher) prefer to keep parents informed about a child's progress or problems?

If conference time is limited (as in most open-house situations when teachers must meet briefly with all the parents), include only those issues that are of particular concern to you, based upon the needs of your child. And try to arrange for both you and your spouse to attend the conference. Not only does it send a message about parental solidarity to your child, it is far more effective when you both hear the information at the same time so there is no room for misinterpretation in the retelling.

GOING BACK TO FOURTH GRADE, TWENTY YEARS LATER
"It didn't surprise me to get a phone call from Shawna's new teacher," said Lyle, the father of four young daughters. "Shawna was always a talker. She was always impulsive. And she always has been a little rebellious about authority. It's been difficult for her to put a lid on it in the classroom. But when I got to the parent-teacher conference, I started to wonder who the real problem was. The teacher would not come out from behind the desk. And when I took the seat she offered me, I was sitting at least four feet below her. It was like I was back in the fourth grade. This teacher literally talked down to me as if I were not on her level!"

Through it all, Lyle remained good-natured. "Maybe that's the only way she feels she can keep unruly parents under control . . . who knows. But one thing's for sure—I didn't stick around long enough to find out."

There are many reasons why a parent-teacher conference seems so unnerving. For one thing, it is never easy to hear a less-than-glowing evaluation of the child you love. And whether we are parents or teachers, it can be difficult for us as humans to take "constructive criticism" or unsolicited advice as something other than a personal attack. But most of all, what makes going back to school such a heavy burden is the weight of all the emotional baggage we have accumulated over the past twenty years.

Who doesn't recall sitting in the principal's office as a child, waiting to receive either a reward or a reprimand? Who among us hasn't passed a sweat-sogged note from teacher to parent, wondering all the while whether he hadn't somehow abetted the delivery of his own death warrant? Nor do these feelings of dread disappear (like a bad guidance counselor) the instant we are accepted to college. No! They come rushing back the moment a teacher summons us into the office for a meeting regarding our child, or when we suddenly find ourselves on the receiving end of a sweaty, dog-eared note.

All of this goes to show you: childhood isn't just a phase of life, it's a state of mind. And no matter what we do or who we become, any feelings of helplessness, powerlessness, or fear we associate with our school years will linger forever in our memories—like the smell of cafeteria peanut butter cookies. But when a teacher uses those feelings to intimidate parents, she loses touch with her most powerful allies. And when a parent responds to a conference invitation with suspicion, defensiveness, and even guilt, he loses an opportunity to become a true and active partner in his child's education.

All of us—parents and teachers alike—enter the school building with our own baggage in tow. (You can get in

160

touch with yours by filling out the inventory in Chapter 5.) But that doesn't mean that that baggage must become a barrier to parent-teacher communication. If you begin the conference by complimenting the teacher on what she's doing right, for instance, it will make it easier for her to accept your complaints or listen to your problems.

Bear in mind that no matter how sensitive you may be to the teacher's feelings, she may be threatened by your message—or by your delivery. It's a good idea, then, to keep your message focused on the problem. Don't start sentences with the word *you*. It will only tempt you to attribute blame. If your child is having problems and you feel the need to complain about a specific technique or teaching method, address the teacher as you would a partner and a respected professional. Ask what she can do to help solve the problem and then follow up by finding out how you can augment her plan at home. Let the teacher know that you are both on the same side when it comes to your child's education: the child's side.

If the conference has been called by your child's teacher, and it is she who has a complaint to voice about your child's attitude or behavior, don't take it as an attack on your ability to parent. Defuse the situation by asking her what she is doing to meet your child's individual needs in the classroom. Then ask to be notified periodically about how things are going, positively as well as negatively.

If her point of view is based on a misconception (if, for instance, she implies that your son is simply not trying to complete his reading assignments), offer specific evidence in your child's behalf (e.g., projects done for extra credit; books read as a family, or as research into those subjects he finds most interesting). If, after much discussion, you are in disagreement with your child's teacher, remind her that you want to be considered her partner in your child's education but that you would prefer an objective opinion on the situation. Don't criticize her opinion or allow her to belittle yours. Instead, agree on an immediate plan of action to tide your child over until parent and teacher can meet again. Then arrange for the principal, counselor, school psychologist, or another neutral party to sit in on the meeting and mediate any remaining points of conflict.

Finally, explain to your child what happened at the meeting. Delineate clearly his role in the solution of the problem (e.g., "From now on, I expect you to complete your reading assignments on time. Until you do, there will be no television or outside play. If you need any help or if you feel that you are falling behind, I will be here for you, as will your teacher."). And whether you agree with the teacher or not, be sure that your child knows that parent and teacher will be in constant touch. It will keep him from playing one side against the other—and keep you from using your child to get at a teacher whose policies you disagree with.

THE GOOD, THE BAD, AND THE INTOLERABLE

In October, Ricky came home with some happy news: because he was performing so well in math, he would be included in a special math enrichment class that met once a week in lieu of his regular class. Things went well until the day his first advanced class was scheduled—and his regular teacher had to let him go.

"Mr. Geoffrey said that I didn't really belong in advanced," sobbed Ricky when he got home. "He said that I would just hold everyone in advanced math back—and that I was making it hard for him by asking for special privileges."

Bonnie was a charming second grader with big brown eyes. But every Monday morning those eyes seemed to fill with tears.

Her mother begged, cajoled, and pleaded for Bonnie to tell her what was the matter. Finally, she did.

"Ms. Roberts yells and yells all day long. Sometimes she yells so much, she makes me feel sick in my stomach."

"I don't have any homework," announced Brian. "We had a sub again today."

A substitute teacher, *again?* Brian's mother shook her head. It seemed to her that Brian was having substitute teachers so often that his regular teacher, Mr. Earlick, would have seemed like a breath of fresh air.

Disturbed by what she considered to be a lack of continuity in Brian's education, his mother began to poll the teachers she knew. What she found was even more disturbing. Mr. Earlick began teaching in 1959. Now sixty-one years old and looking forward to retirement, Edward Earlick had accumulated eighty-six sick days. According to a fellow teacher, his intention was to take all of them before he retired. That way he could spend as little time as possible at school but still "hang on" until he reached his sixty-fifth birthday.

In a recent poll, six out of ten adult Americans said that one particular teacher was caring enough and talented enough to make a substantial difference in their lives. With a little luck and some help from you, your child may be discovering that caring, talented teacher for herself in her very own classroom this year.

But experience doesn't always make the best teacher. If what a teacher encounters on a daily basis is an uncontrolled school system, an uncaring principal, disinterested students, and parents who are disinclined to help, his experiences are bound to mar his attitude toward the students he teaches and taint the way that he teaches them.

Most of the time, teacher-student personality conflicts can be worked out easily if they are honestly addressed in conference. But on occasion, a teacher becomes entrenched—both in his job and in his feelings of anger, paranoia, or apathy. It isn't easy for a parent to take a teacher to task on the basis of his personality or professional adequacy. But when a teacher's attitude becomes a threat to a student's ego or academic status, it is a parent's *duty* to take immediate action.

The main challenge in dealing justly with an angry or frightened teacher is not controlling him but controlling yourself. We can all be tempted to give as good as we get, especially when a child's welfare hangs in the balance. But a teacher who yells at a child isn't just a problem teacher—he is a teacher with a problem. Unless we keep the situation cool, we cannot hope to find a solution. For that reason, it is crucial that the meeting include one or more objective mediators—such as the school principal or psychologist.

Nor are you likely to discover the root of the problem without hearing the other side of the story—the side only your child can tell. Indeed, having a conference about your child without including him in it is like reading about a piece of art that you have never seen: you may be getting all of the substance but none of the visuals. Encourage your child to become a part of the discussion.

Does his story change in the presence of the principal? Does he seem uptight? Is he having trouble staying in his seat? If so, he may genuinely fear the teacher—or he may be fearing that any embellishments he has added to the story are about to be found out.

As a parent, you may not be comfortable with the idea of allowing children in on "adult conversations." But there are other good reasons for allowing the student and teacher to meet face-to-face. Such an encounter keeps teacher and student from telling tales behind each other's backs. It keeps you—the parent—from telling the child's story for him (and perhaps adding some embellishments of your own). It makes any "chemical dislike" that exists between teacher and student obvious and observable to the mediators. And, if it is handled with sensitivity, it makes it possible for all the "injured" parties to tell their story, explain their attitudes, and "save face" by focusing not on individual problems but on a mutually acceptable solution.

WHEN ALL ELSE FAILS

"My father has always been right on target when it comes to my daughter, Jody," Jody's mother, Louise, reported. "He always said that 'Jody could talk the horns off a billy goat.' And I told Jody's teacher as much. But when Jody told us that her teacher punished her by making her write 'I will not disrupt the class' a hundred times, I thought I was doing everyone a favor by scheduling a conference. I had to let her teacher know that we don't approve of using writing as a punishment. We feel that it gives a child the wrong impression of school skills.

"Everything seemed all right until a few weeks later. Jody had a comment to make about what was going on in science class, and she just couldn't keep it in. Ms. Wright, her teacher, flew into a rage. 'You've disturbed the entire class,' she screamed. 'Now you'll have to see the principal. You see, I don't *dare* punish you on my own.' "

If, after the first conference, your child comes home upset by a teacher's excessive screaming, if the teacher is absent excessively, or if your child has been singled out for punitive action, don't quietly remove your child from that teacher's class (leaving him to work out his aggressions on the remaining children)—go straight to the principal with your complaints. The stress of the job may be too heavy a burden for the teacher to bear. He may need to transfer to a different kind of school. He may even need to take a leave of absence.

If you are dissatisfied with the outcome of your meeting with the principal, you may take your complaint to the superintendent or school board—but only after you take a moment to consider whether you have made your child's cause your personal vendetta. Certainly, you want to save your child a great deal of grief—but have you given any thought to saving what might be an otherwise good teacher's professional reputation? The teacher may be a different person once your child is out of the classroom. She may be teaching a subject she is not confident about—or frustrated by a haphazard school system.

Teaching and parenting are two of the hardest jobs there are. Yet it is the meshing of these two roles that is at the very heart of the educational process. Before you ask for a teacher's head, be sure your head and heart are in the right place. Better yet, deal with these problems before they start—by becoming a positive force in your child's education.

A dedicated teacher can shed a great deal of light on the independent life your child leads outside the home. But no one knows your child better than *you* do! Ask any dedicated, professional educator and she will tell you that your insight can be the key that unlocks your child's potential—and the secret to keeping student-teacher relations happy.

What can you teach the teacher about the little person who has become your most interesting and challenging subject? Plenty . . . for instance:

- *The secret of his learning style.* A child who turns off a lecture after the first five minutes will ultimately do a crash-and-burn if his teacher tends to be verbal. Likewise, a tactile learner won't learn much if he is asked to absorb his lessons through reading rather than hands-on methods.

  Denying a child the opportunity to learn the way he prefers to learn is a surefire way to turn a discovery process into an interminable source of frustration.

  To discover what learning style your child prefers, watch what he does with an exciting new piece of information. If he writes about it or draws a picture of it, he is visual. If he talks about it (straight through dinner and right up until bedtime), he may literally be talking his way into learning. If he wants to explore it physically, he may be a physical or motoric learner.

- *His personal style.* Little Marta, an only child, seemed to be constantly complaining about her teacher. To hear Marta tell it, Ms. Blanchard "was angry all the time," a condition that caused Marta considerable emotional discomfort. When Marta's mother visited the classroom, she immediately zeroed in on the problem. Ms. Blanchard wasn't "yelling" and she wasn't "angry"—she simply had a louder, more robust speaking style than either of Marta's parents.

Even as adults, we are all taken aback by people whose emotions are not easily read. Left on her own, Marta may have gone through the entire school year feeling distracted and even somewhat disoriented. But because her mother was sensitive to her own personal style as well as to Ms. Blanchard's, she was able to explain the difference away.

- *Your child's interests.* Let the teacher know what your child is interested in, and you have given her a veritable roadmap to all the inroads to learning. A girl who lives from one ballet lesson to the next but is having trouble reading may jump into that subject if she is given a book about young dancers. Likewise, a boy who is doing poorly in math may find it easier to catch on if his teacher uses a favorite toy—such as Lego—to illustrate his point.

This advice, of course, relies heavily on the assumption that we know what our kids are all about—and that assumption, unfortunately, is not always true. Parents have a tendency to define children in comparative terms. Compared to his sibling, he is the "quiet one." She may be the "oldest of the cousins" or "the family scholar." Together they may even be "the instigators." But how many of us have taken the time to discover our children for the unique individuals they are?

Left on his own, what does your son like to do? What kind of music does he prefer? What's your daughter's favorite color? If you weren't around and she could go anywhere she wanted, where would she go? What toy would she take with her?

This kind of information may not seem as crucial to you as a standardized test score or report card grade, but it can net a teacher more and deeper knowledge than she will ever get from your child's grades.

And there's an added plus: the more you and the teacher learn about your child, the more you will learn about parent-teacher partnership. And that's the kind of experience that can make *any* teacher a better teacher.

9
Special Help for Your Special Child

"Do you want to know how important you are? You are the most important person in this room. In fact, this meeting is all about you! Your parents, your teacher, and your counselor are all here to find out what you do well—and you do a lot of things well. We're also going to find out what makes you so special: how you learn the way you learn, and how we can help you with those things that you find more difficult."

In this way, using these very words, we have introduced hundreds of children to the fascinating and frustrating learner within. What makes that learner fascinating is his ability to latch on to certain bits of information and hold them firmly in his memory. What can make him frustrating is the way other lessons, no matter how carefully taught, seem to elude his grasp.

This chapter is not about convincing you that costly special education programs, bilingual education, gifted and talented programs, or remedial programs are indispensable. Nor is it an attempt to assuage those parents who believe that in public schools the "average learner" is being overlooked. Its purpose is to make you see public education as a system that educates millions of individuals, many of whom learn in different ways than others.

BILINGUAL EDUCATION

Some children in public elementary school speak a language other than English. Although some of them may know a few words of English, they simply don't "think in it" the way they do their first language. School systems offer bilingual education programs to allow these children to enjoy the same basic privilege that English-speaking children enjoy: to learn the basics of reading, math, and language arts in their first, and more comfortable, language.

The way most bilingual programs work is this: Linguistically diverse children in grades one through six have a certain percentage of their instruction taught to them in their native language and a certain percentage taught in English. In first grade, the ratio is approximately 80:20, with their first language being used the most. By third or fourth grade, the ratio is reversed, to 20:80. Ultimately, the children are integrated or mainstreamed (either in part or fully) into an all English-speaking curriculum.

But the great controversy about bilingual education is not how quickly these children are assimilated into the mainstream culture but whether bilingual education should exist at all. We have all heard the doughnut shop regulars telling one another how their parents had come from Poland, Norway, Italy, or Germany, speaking little or no English. Somehow they made it through school in an all English-speaking class. If they could do it, "these people" should be able to do it too.

171

Times have changed. "Making it," even in elementary school, is a great deal more complex today than it was two generations ago. And educators know more about the psychological and financial implications of prejudice and cultural isolation than ever before. They have seen how immersing a five-year-old in an alien culture is like throwing a child into water to force him to learn to swim. And they have learned that when most children are thrown into a pool of academic and social confusion, they are at great risk of drowning.

But the home remains the heart of learning. Until a child's parents are mainstreamed, she cannot be expected to be successfully integrated, academically or socially. If your child is taking part in a bilingual program, it is critical that both parents—and the rest of the family—learn English. It is the only way you can truly participate in your child's school life.

Nor should you consider an extended stay in a bilingual program a benefit—or an emotional tie to your culture. School systems that keep students in bilingual programs for five, six, or even ten years because of politics, prejudice, or poor educational programs only render a terrible disservice to linguistically diverse students. If your child has been in a bilingual program for more than three years without other extenuating circumstances, it is time for you to ask for an explanation. A child can be successfully mainstreamed into society only if she is first successfully mainstreamed in school. It is your responsibility to act as your child's advocate.

THE GIFTED AND TALENTED PROGRAM

Is it right to include the academically gifted in the special needs category? As one specialist at the Hollingworth Center for Highly Gifted Children put it, "Highly gifted children are as far from the norm in the direction of giftedness as the severely [learning disabled] are in the other direction."

Yet the ways in which we select our academically gifted children have recently come under fire—as have our methods for providing them with an enriching and challenging educational experience. Across the nation, gifted and talented programs are under budgetary attack. Legislators, faced with dramatic budget shortfalls, are finding it more difficult than ever to support special ed programs for those in need. Increasingly, they are leaving our bright students to grab a book and "enrich themselves." Heterogeneous learning groups are quickly replacing G & T "pull out" programs, to many parents' dismay. And even educators have begun to wonder aloud whether "giftedness" is really measurable, whether average students (who tend to fare better in school) are being overlooked—and whether the designation "gifted" is just another word for "elitist."

BESTOWING GIFTEDNESS

Although the existence of the G & T program is widespread, there are no generally accepted criteria for choosing which students are best suited for the program—nor are there any guidelines designating who is best qualified to make that decision. In fact, the criteria for identifying "gifts" and "talents" are so frustratingly elusive that a "gifted" student who transfers from one school system to another cannot be assured that his designation will make the move along with him.

For the sake of research (and, occasionally, for the sake of keeping the peace at the PTO), some educators define the academically gifted student as one who has scored at least 140 on an IQ test or a student who has proven himself a prodigy in one or more academic subjects. But IQ tests are by no means infallible. Sometimes, the extraordinarily bright child may read too much into test questions, thus skewing his answers. Sometimes a talented student's potential is masked by a learning difficulty. And, as critics argue, the cultural bias built into such tests can keep the gifts of black, Hispanic, and female students from shining through.

But the biggest obstacles to defining *giftedness* can be the kids themselves. No one ever said that gifted children are also disciplined. Good study habits, after all, are not an inborn trait. Otherwise bright children who do not turn in their homework or participate in class may find themselves weeded out during the selection process. And contrary to popular playground belief, extremely bright children do not automatically fit into the "goody two shoes" mold. Gifted students often find repetitive classwork boring. As a result, they can become disruptive, inattentive, or even behavior problems.

Finally, there is the stigma of "nerdiness." Primary school children don't hesitate to call a dweeb a dweeb. As a result, many of our brightest boys and girls hide their talents under a Bart Simpson T-shirt just to fit in with the popular crowd. In all, some educators estimate that there are as many as six to ten times the number of "gifted" children in our schools as previously estimated.

GETTING WITH THE PROGRAM

Nancy was a nurse. She was also nursing a complaint against her daughter Jessica's school.

"Jessie takes piano lessons. Her instructor has called her talented. She has even made up little tunes all by herself," Nancy huffed. "So why didn't she get into the gifted and talented program? Answer me *that*."

* * *

We have answered many parents like Nancy. And although our response sounds like a bromide, it is one to which we have dedicated our careers. We believe that every child is, in one way or another, gifted or talented. We also believe that the singlemost goal underlying the parent-teacher partnership is to allow each child to explore the talent he has to its fullest potential; to be empowered by it, and to use it to empower others. But a child will never fulfill his potential until we stop demanding that he fulfill our expectations.

That is easier said than done. Every parent thinks of his child as genius material. Every mother marvels at her son's facility with numbers or her daughter's ability to argue a point like a supreme court justice. That is why we wonder, when our young scholar is not among the chosen, whether the school has missed something in its evaluation. And we wonder whether our child will be missing something too. After all, if gifted children are "challenged," what does that mean for an average learner? That she will be left to languish? If gifted kids are expected to be bright, are average students perceived as dull? And if whiz kids are taught by a "gifted and talented teacher," who will be instructing the others?

Oftentimes, fears like these are rooted in our own experiences. In the past, gifted children were not so carefully chosen as they are now. And many G & T programs were blatantly elitist. Those designated as gifted were routinely isolated from the rest of the student body, as though averageness were a disease they might catch. But that is not the case now.

Though programs for the gifted vary from town to town, they share one very important goal: inclusion. Ideally, the very bright child remains in the standard classroom where he can inspire his peers—and learn from them as well. Then, once or twice a week, he may be taken out of the classroom to participate in accelerated projects, field trips, advanced approaches to learning, dramatics, critical review of reading material, computer analysis, and the arts—all under the watchful eye of a specialized teacher. Upon his return, the G & T child can share his new knowledge with others—just as the other children will share their knowledge, hobbies, and social skills with him. In that way, he remains an active part of the classroom culture. He is valued not because of what he knows, but because of who he is.

In some schools, up to half the class of children has been designated gifted while the other half participates in the standard curriculum. Obviously, it takes a talented teacher to be able to promote overall class spirit, challenge all students, and do what it takes to make the model work. But it can be done. In fact, it's being done in classrooms from Maine to California.

IS MY CHILD ACADEMICALLY GIFTED?

As a rule, parents and teachers have a hint that a child is extraordinarily bright long before the formal identification process begins. She may display wonderful analytical skills, mastering shape sorters and zipping through puzzles nearly as fast as you can provide them. He may spend his quiet afternoons writing and illustrating stories that amaze us. She may read with comprehension when she is four or take to a computer like a duck to water.

If you have reason to believe that your child is academically gifted (and remember—parental pride is not reason enough!), you should contact his teacher or the school principal. Ask them what programs for gifted children are offered in your school system. If you live in a town that does not have a formal program, you can urge the school board to develop one.

Meanwhile, you can see to it that your child is given

a learning experience that is both challenging and nurturing by following these guidelines:

- *Offer him "enrichment" in the course of everyday life.* Take advantage of story hour at the local library—then ask the librarian if he will demonstrate how the card stamper works. Bake cookies, then deliver them to the local nursing home. Plant bulbs, then wait for them to come up the following spring. Pleasurable activities like these encourage a child to learn without pressure— and they give busy parents a chance to stop and smell the flowers too.

- *Encourage her to find a social group in which she feels comfortable.* You may be directing your child toward a same-age peer group, but she may find older children—or a mixed group—more stimulating. Let her decide where she fits in.

- *Remember that even gifted children can be turned off to school.* Ask the teacher whether broadening the curriculum can help. If she agrees to provide a faster flow and range of information, or allows a range of learning methods, your G & T kid is more likely to stay challenged. If, for instance, the class is learning about dinosaurs, your gifted child can do additional research or perhaps a video. That way, a bright child is not bored, and his classmates are enriched by his efforts.

- *Think twice about allowing your child to skip a grade level.* Your gifted child may be reading beyond his age level, but he has not developed the social skills he will need to succeed with older kids. Enrichment programs, on the other hand, benefit the whole child.

- *Don't teach your gifted child to be elitist.* You may acknowledge that the class benefits from contact with your bright children but only if you also acknowledge that your child benefits from contact with the class.

- *Be aware that gifted children are not immune to learning difficulties*. In fact, high intelligence can make diagnosis more difficult since bright children can more easily compensate for common learning difficulties like those described in the next section.

LEARNING DIFFICULTIES

Hold a magazine up to a mirror and try to read it. "Watch" television with a towel covering the screen. Try drawing a map to your house with your opposite hand—then ask someone to follow the directions you have written. Sound difficult? You're right. And they're just some of the frustrations that 20 percent of American children—those who must struggle with learning difficulties—face daily.

Because learning difficulties come in many forms, parents don't often think of challenged kids as having much in common—but they do. Whether they are troubled by what we call dyslexia or challenged by Attention Deficit Hyperactive Disorder (ADHD), children with learning difficulties may find it hard to master the basics. And although learning difficulties can erode self-confidence, LD kids often feel smarter than their grades indicate— and many times, they are! It is not uncommon for them to have IQs in the normal to high intelligence range. What *is* uncommon is the way they prefer to learn. And until we discover that, they are no more likely to make an educational breakthrough than they are to break through a stone wall with their bare hands. We are asking them to perform tasks without giving them the tools they need to accomplish them.

Brian was not a strong reader. But he had never had problems with math until he reached the third grade—and Mr. Carew's class.

At first, his parents were shocked. Brian's in-school exercises were either turned in incomplete or were totally incorrect. Finally, he began refusing to participate in Mr. Carew's class.

Yet when he reworked his math problems at home—on the small blackboard in his room—Brian seemed at ease with his work. He even seemed to enjoy it!

Brian's parents pointed out the discrepancy to the school principal, who promised to sit in on a couple of his classes. It was then that Brian's anxious parents learned the truth: when Mr. Carew taught a lesson to his third graders, he never used the blackboard as a "visual." Instead, he asked the class to follow along as he read the directions and example from the text.

Because Brian was not a strong reader, he simply could not absorb the textual lesson. And without visual clues, like the ones his parents had provided on the blackboard, he was completely lost. This kind of lesson wasn't teaching Brian anything about math. It was only reinforcing how much trouble he had with reading.

Every one of us has a preferred learning style. To see it in action, all we have to do is pay attention to our automatic response when someone gives us information to process, like a phone number. Those of us who prefer hearing our input will repeat the number to ourselves until we commit it to memory. Those of us who, like Brian, prefer a visual presentation, will scrawl it on a pad.

But for every method of learning for which we have a

preference, there is also a learning style that does not come so naturally. It is as though there is a wiring problem in the brain that affects the way we process information. That is what we mean by a learning difficulty. In time, some of us learn to cope with our LDs, either compensating for them or overcoming them. But left undiagnosed and untreated, severe learning difficulties can erode a student's confidence and, ultimately, turn the learning process into a painful experience.

DIAGNOSIS

Learning disabilities often are so subtle it is difficult to diagnose them. A child might seek out and excel in subjects that are not so profoundly affected by the disability. The subtle LD may even be incorrectly tagged a behavior problem or immaturity.

But more profound LDs can sometimes be marked at an early age. The child may be slow to speak, slow to respond, or unable to recall the directions given to her only a few moments before. When the child begins to read, she may be reading *d* when others see *b*. Or she might not be able to understand what numbers symbolize. Or, she may simply be unable to manipulate a pencil.

By now, we have all come to know the symptoms of such common LDs as dyslexia, hyperactivity, and lack of motor control. It is only human for us to see these evidences and respond defensively, fending off our suspicions with phrases like "He's not really trying" or "So she just doesn't have great penmanship; neither do most doctors." We may even know parents who have gone through the testing process only to find it more emotionally draining than the LD itself. Nevertheless, it is obviously in the child's best interest to diagnose LDs as quickly as possible.

"I know James can't sit still," complained Laura, his weary mother. "But what seven-year-old kid can? I thought he was supposed to be full of energy. I thought he was supposed to be full of life. Then I get this note from his teacher." She waved the paper helplessly. "Where am I supposed to draw the line between normal behavior and problem behavior? And since when have the characteristics of normal, happy kids become *symptoms*?"

Since parents and teachers have become so familiar with the effects of LDs on a child's educational potential and self-esteem, we perhaps have been a little too suspicious about the boy who can't hold a pen correctly or the girl who just can't "get" long division.

Still, it is not the behavior but the degree of the behavior that counts. If you or your child's teacher notice that he is not keeping pace in a certain subject, he may simply lack talent or interest in that area. But if he exhibits several of the following symptoms, it may be time to decide whether an evaluation is in order:

- *General difficulty with language*. This can include problems with speech or language acquisition in the preschool period as well as difficulties with reading and spelling thereafter. Testing can reveal whether the problem is in the input or output end of the learning process.

- *Difficulty with writing*. Handwriting may be illegible. Block letters may be combined with cursive. The child may forget midword how to finish it. Letters may be reversed or omitted. Providing her with a computer or typewriter may help to tap the information stored in her brain.

- *Difficulty with math*. He may seem perplexed by the concept of numbers, stymied by the order involved in counting, or simply confused by "too many numbers."

- *Problems with attentiveness*. These may range from chronic "inattentiveness" (the marked inability to concentrate on a lesson), to lack of focus, to boredom leading to disruptive behavior in class.

- *Inability to control small movements*. Examples of small movements are the pincer grasp and the fine finger manipulations involved in writing.

Once the problem is brought to everyone's attention, a meeting should be scheduled to discuss it. At that time, everyone who is involved with your child—his classroom teacher, counselor, perhaps the learning difficulties tutor or speech therapist, and you—is invited to voice his or her concerns and opinions. The staff specialists may suggest that classroom adaptations (such as increased remedial help) be made in order to see whether that would alleviate the problem. If, on the other hand, the group decides that further evaluation is needed, parents are advised of their rights, asked for written permission, and the evaluation process begins. Since it is part of the federally mandated school services, the evaluation is free.

In many ways, the evaluation process is like drawing a map. We begin where the child is, then trace the problem back to its roots. Later, parents and teachers can use the same map to guide them as they chart a course toward a probable solution. This is not to say that there are not a good many stop-offs and detours along the way. It's just too bad that so many of those detours seem to lead to guilt, embarrassment, defensiveness, and anger.

For most of us, our families are the heart and soul of our lives. They are the tender core around which we build a shell of privacy and love. It is our instinct—and usually our best interest—to protect those whom we hold dear. Yet the instant we agree to cooperate with a special services evaluation, our lives become an open book. Before we really know what hit us, the education specialist, who may also be the learning disabilities tutor, has administered achievement tests and a learning disability test battery to our child. The speech therapist, who specializes in auditory processing, will also test our child. The psychologist has evaluated the child's psychological status, tested his IQ, and taken a complete medical and developmental history (including any incidents in pregnancy that might have affected the child's development). Meanwhile, the classroom teacher is busily compiling her observations of our child in the classroom. Worse, the entire process often includes a visit from the social worker—a visit even the best parents may find intimidating. Take, for example, the reactions of Linda.

Linda is a pediatrician in a well-to-do town. She was also a happy, confident parent who was coping quite well with the speech problems of her daughter, Evelyn—until Evelyn stopped making progress and the in-depth evaluation process began. "We dealt fairly well with the physical examinations. We even breezed right through the psychological testing. But when the social worker came to visit our home, something inside me just cracked. I felt like he was second-guessing everything I had ever done as a parent. The next thing I knew, I was feeling guilty. I'm a doctor, for Pete's sake! Why couldn't I help my daughter with her problem? Did I *cause* it?"

All things considered, we think that Linda has held together miraculously well. Most parents can't help but feel they are being swept along by a process they cannot control. And they can't help but cringe at the thought that every decision they made in their child's life is now being scrutinized. They spend their days hoping that it will all go away—and their nights wondering whether they are genetically or psychologically to blame for a child's LD.

These worries and self-doubts may be especially haunting for the parents of those children who are challenged by what is perhaps the most misunderstood of all the learning difficulties: Attention Deficit Hyperactive Disorder. Often tagged a behavior or inattention problem, ADHD is a physiological disorder that makes it impossible for a child to keep his mind focused on a lesson. The child cannot concentrate and becomes bored. He may then relieve his boredom by becoming a disruptive force in the classroom.

Coping with ADHD can be a challenge to every member of the family. Siblings must cope daily with friends and even teachers who remark, "I hope you're not anything like your brother." Parents are unable to control their child—often in full view of irritated teachers and critical relatives. In time, they become so frustrated by the child's behavior that they swear they will do *anything* to put an end to it. Until they begin to weigh the benefits and dangers of medication.

Learning difficulties—all of them—can create in a family a great deal of guilt, ambivalence, and anger. Even the research—especially those studies indicating a "genetic link"—can make good parents wonder whether they haven't inadvertently programmed their children for failure.

But parents are not responsible for a child's learning difficulties. In fact, they are critical components in the process of reeducating the child to his potential and his abilities. And that job begins when the evaluation team has completed its study.

Within thirty school days from the time parents give written permission for the evaluation, parents, teachers, and specialists come together once again to go over the tests and findings. (Brace yourself—the amount of information you will receive in this one day may be staggering.) Then, as a group, you will decide what special services will benefit your child most: extra help in the standard classroom; a teacher and specialist team in the classroom; tutoring in areas of difficulty in a small-class setting; or an all-day small-class setting from which the child may be mainstreamed in gym, music, art.

If you disagree with the findings of the team, your child need not live with the consequences. You are entitled by Public Law 94-142 to seek an independent, outside evaluation for which the school system will pay. Likewise, if you do not agree with the individualized education plan suggested by the group, you need not suffer in silence. If the differences cannot be worked out within the school system, a mediator from the state will hear both sides of the case and rule on the hearing. Nor should you worry that your child will be designated as "special needs" forever. Your child's plan must be reviewed annually. After three years, if your child continues to receive special services, a reevaluation will be done to determine whether he has achieved his educational objectives. If he has, new objectives can be set—or special education services can be discontinued.

SMOOTHING OUT THE LEARNING LOOP

The learning process can be visualized as a loop. In that loop, *input,* or information, is taken in or collected in the brain. (For instance, the child picks up a block.) The information is then *integrated,* or sorted, by the brain. (It may be classified as red, wooden, square.) Later, when the information is *processed,* the child stores the information he has picked up about the block. When he needs to, he can *output* what he has learned, either orally (telling you about the block) or visually (drawing a picture of it).

A difficulty in one of these four areas (input, integration, processing, or output) is like a twist in the learning loop. The learner either can't take in what is seen or heard, or can't put forth the information taken in.

But there is a great deal a parent can do to smooth the path to learning for the LD child, especially while an individualized education plan is in action:

- *Make allowances for learning difficulties.* A child may not be able to control a pencil, but she is in full control of her faculties! Don't let her fail because of her penmanship. Ask her teacher whether she might type rather than write her assignments—or, if no keyboard is available, to give reports orally.

- *Lobby for mainstreaming in your school.* A classroom made up of the gifted and talented, average learners, challenged learners, and bilingual students is an invaluable replica of the real world. Besides, isolation deprives children of one very important way to learn: by modeling.

- *Ask the teacher to allow your child to sit in the front of the room.* This simple change can help some students focus their attention.

- *Suggest that your son write his class notes on every other line of his notebook.* This makes notes easier to read and eliminates the confusion of overcrowded pages.

- *Use tracking to prevent sensory overload*. The LD child often finds it difficult to see the forest for the trees— or the individual words in a mass of sentences. Don't let him be overwhelmed by a page full of symbols. Instead, have him cover with a piece of paper all but the line he is reading. It will enable him to "track" across the page step by step, much the same way a horse tracks around a racecourse. (Without a track, on the other hand, horses will run randomly, making no progress.)

- *Color code class notes*. This is done to call attention to topics of special importance or those that need reinforcement. (One child with Attention Deficit reported that he learned to memorize his notes photographically. That way, he could call up the "look" of an entire page of material—in visual form—rather than the information itself.)

- *Give your child a tape recorder to take to school*. Tape recorders are now small enough and inconspicuous enough to fit in a child's pocket. They can be a boon to kids who prefer to learn aurally (through hearing).

- *Get to know the preferred learning styles of all your children, whether or not they show evidence of learning difficulty*. A child who puts her hands over her ears may be sensitive to auditory stimulation, but a kid who does homework with the radio blasting is not likely to be stimulated by talk.

- *Provide a variety of learning options to improve your child's chances of success*. Don't keep drilling a child who is weak in phonics in his area of weakness. Instead, let him absorb phonics while doing something he enjoys, like reading about dinosaurs, for instance. Or give him project-oriented work (like painting and labeling

187

pictures of dinosaurs) until he feels more comfortable as a successful learner.

- *Don't try to keep the disability a deep, dark secret.* Siblings can help support an LD brother or sister if they are in the know. Kids *always* suspect when something is going on. Left to imagine the worst, the LD child may come to believe that there is something so terribly wrong with him that even his parents can't talk about it! Let him off the hook by letting him in on the fact that he learns differently than other kids—and that you are doing everything you can to help him succeed.

PAC GROUPS

Every time a school system receives state or federal monies on behalf of special education children, a parents' advisory (PAC) group must be set up to oversee the spending of those monies. This group not only feeds back information to the agency that supports it but helps formulate special ed policy for the school. Since PAC groups are made up mainly of parents whose kids are currently receiving special ed services, they can be of great help to parents of newly enrolled students—and an ongoing source of support and information throughout the school year.

AVERAGE LEARNERS

Developing curriculum is a thankless task. The educators who define what our children will learn are inevitably taken to task, either by those critics who believe they are catering to the unique needs of the gifted, special needs, or bilingual population, or by those who feel that most students are being cheated by a curriculum that is too "middle-of-the-road." The truth is that the curriculum offered at each grade level is geared to the average ability of most students. When new or revised texts are written, they are field tested (put in the hands of those who will use them) to make sure that they are neither too easy nor too hard.

In our years in education, we have discovered that the word *average* is a misnomer when it comes to children. But this is the challenge we face when it comes to enriching those multitalented, multidimensional students who tend to earn *Bs* and *Cs* in schoolwork. Average learners have academic strengths and weaknesses (as do the gifted)—but posing too much of a challenge in any one subject can make them feel inadequate and turn them off to learning. They may be motivated in the subjects that interest them, but in those classes where motivation is minimal, you may find them on cloud nine.

BRINGING STUDENTS DOWN TO EARTH
Bobby, a fifth grader, always seemed to get off to a great start in September. His father, Robert, knew exactly what to expect when he brought home his first report card of the year. It was always *Bs* and *Cs*. Unfortunately, Robert also knew what to expect as the school year wore on. Bobby was prone to the winter blahs. As February blew in, his energy level always seemed to blow out. And this year was no exception.

"I knew what the note from Bobby's teacher was going to say even before I opened it," said Robert. "Bobby never seemed to have homework. He never seemed to have tests to study for. Instead of cracking the books, he spent every night in front of the Nintendo." Robert sighed. "Too bad they don't give tests in Super Mario II. Bobby would be a straight *A* student."

Maybe schools don't give tests in video games—but teachers from coast to coast *are* using the current computer game craze to shake students like Bobby out of their doldrums. According to the Center for Research on Elementary and Middle Schools at the Johns Hopkins University, 96 percent of all schools nationwide have made computers a part of their curriculum. But if the computers or computer learning programs in your schools are reserved for the gifted or used as rewards, it is time to remind your child's teacher of this simple fact: average students may be only moderately motivated about school-work, but they are wild about video games.

How do computers enhance learning for the average student? They demystify technology, thus preparing young students for an increasingly electronic future. They make lessons seem real. The child stops thinking of problem solving, estimating, basic math, and cause and effect as nebulous theory. These are the skills he can plug in to win interactive adventure games. Most of all, computers (and lively software) can make old lessons new, reviving a child's sense of excitement about school and learning.

Are the computers in your child's classroom being put to the best possible use? You can be sure they are if you:

- *Ask for the earliest possible computer instruction*. In a recent nationwide survey of teachers, 41 percent said that computer instruction should begin no later than first grade.

- *Make sure computers are considered part of the total educational journey*. Computer science is a necessary course of study. It puts the tools of computer usage into your child's hands. But if you show a child how computers can be used to learn such subjects as science, social studies, math, or reading, you set a child free to explore and experiment at his own pace.

- *Check out the software in the classroom*. Drills and

repetitive teaching methods are never fun—even if they come from a computer. Suggest that your teacher try an interactive disk instead. These require logic and imagination to solve. And take advantage of any additional features the computer might offer, such as a color monitor or sound. It can be fun to draw a picture of a farm. But to computer-illustrate a barnyard scene, color it electronically, and add the sound of the animals who live there—*that* can be heaven.

THERE IS NO AVERAGE REACTION TO AVERAGE

To some parents, a *C* is a perfectly respectable grade. To others, it is a family catastrophe. To the second group of parents, we offer this gentle reminder: the best way to bring out a talent in a child is by validating that talent. Pressuring the child to bring up his grades or bribing him "to turn that *C* into a *B*" teaches him to pursue a wrongheaded goal—and for all the wrong reasons.

Even the latest of bloomers will blossom if enrichment is made part of his everyday life. In school, that means finding a teacher who knows how to keep a class challenged but not overwhelmed. It means using a hands-on, multisensory approach as an antidote to the passive stimulation that TVs and VCRs provide. And it means opening up in-class learning centers not as rewards but as a source of creative learning for those children who might appreciate it most. Field trips, guest speakers, crafts projects, or rearranging desks will also help keep children interested.

At home, enrichment can be very simple. A quick stop at the post office, a visit to the laundromat, vaccinating a pet, trying on hats, watching clouds, making an omelet—nearly *any* experience can be enriching if it is approached imaginatively.

Just as there are no average children, there are no

routine experiences. Parents and teachers need to offer education in all its richness and diversity if the diverse needs of our "average" learners are going to be met.

MEETING THE CHALLENGE OF A CHANGING WORLD

As we have said, a public school is a microcosm of the community in which it exists. The lawns on your street may be fenced. The houses may be securely locked. But there is nothing that can keep the problems that plague our communities out of our lives—or out of our schools.

In many ways, the programs described above serve as a buffer, protecting our youngest citizens from the effects of prejudice, deprivation, or cultural or intellectual alienation. But for other children—including those who have been prenatally exposed to drugs or alcohol, those who suffer from AIDS or abuse—no formal, federally mandated programs exist.

Nevertheless, educators and parents can do a great deal to mobilize against the illnesses and addictions that threaten our children if they take advantage of the resources provided by our schools.

CHILDREN WHO HAVE BEEN PRENATALLY EXPOSED TO DRUGS

Cocaine and crack addiction reached record proportions in the mid-1980s—and so did the birthrates of drug-exposed children. Now educators across the United States are preparing themselves to deal with the innocent victims of that plague: the first generation of "crack babies" who will enter school this fall.

For the parents of such children, the baby's birth is simply the beginning of the suffering. They must witness their infant's painful withdrawal knowing that they have caused it. Some must entrust their child to foster care.

Others use the infant's struggle for life as the impetus for their own personal struggle. They may even find enough strength in parenthood to finally break their addictions. But that, unfortunately, is not enough to deliver a child from the long-term effects of his parents' dependency.

As researchers have learned, drug-exposed children often sustain long-term damage. And the symptoms of that damage—which include seizures, cerebral palsy, mental retardation, hyperactivity, mood swings, extreme passivity, or a complete lack of emotion—can put a normal learning experience out of reach.

If you are the parent or guardian of such a child, it is imperative that you request a developmental screening as soon as the child reaches the age of three. With the help of professionals, you may be able to alleviate certain deficits, including slow speech development, which is common to drug-exposed children.

When the child enters school, be sure to educate her teacher, principal, and counselor as to her situation even if no symptoms exist. Neither the child's educators nor her parents should accept "normal" test scores or grades as evidence that she is problem-free. Parents and teachers who are lulled by passing grades may fail to seek out subtle LDs, denying the child use of any special services that might help her. (A drug-exposed child may fit into a screener's "idea of normalcy" and escape testing altogether.)

And don't pass off symptoms that are common to drug exposed kids (such as hostility or hyperactivity) as bad behavior. It is imperative that they receive treatment as promptly as possible.

LOW-BIRTHWEIGHT AND PREMATURE BABIES
Many factors can cause low birthweight or premature birth: the use of alcohol during pregnancy, smoking, ex-

posure to drugs, or simply destiny. These infants often experience learning and/or behavioral problems later on. But, as outlined in the June 13, 1990 issue of the *Journal of the American Medical Association*, these fragile babies can become robust learners if educators and parents intervene early.

In an unusually large study, including nearly a thousand children in eight diverse cities, researchers delineated two groups: the early learners (who were treated to language games, and social and intellectual development techniques from birth) and those children who did not receive the services. The results were staggering. In the first three years of their lives, the children who received the intervention raised their IQs by an average of 9.9 points. Moreover, they nearly eliminated the behavioral problems often associated with extremely low birthweight.

If you are the parent of a child whose development has been affected by this condition, it may benefit you to speak with your local school psychologist. He may be able to recommend exercises to stimulate your child's intellectual and developmental growth. Or he can direct you to a specialist who can develop a program specifically for your child. Whatever you do, remember that it is crucial for you to intervene early. What you do in the first years of your child's life could benefit him for a lifetime.

CHILDREN WITH AIDS

Children who have tested positive for the Human Immuno-deficiency Virus have physical, emotional, and psychological needs that go far beyond the reach—or jurisdiction—of the school. Yet there is much a school can do to provide a warm, welcoming environment for the HIV-positive child—and it begins with having a compassionate, comprehensive AIDS policy in place.

Your school, like many others, may have put off such policy making. Because no consistent school guidelines have yet been established, each school district has been left to grapple with the issue individually. Some systems have chosen to remain silent on the issue of HIV-positive teachers or students; others have so far been spared the experience; a minority have met the disease head-on, providing parents, teachers, and students with a clear outline of school policies and procedures.

If you are the parent of an HIV-positive child, it is your responsibility to inform the principal, school psychologist, and your child's teacher about his condition. And it is your right to develop—along with local educators—an AIDS policy to protect your child's privacy, safeguard his health, and defend his right to learn in a standard classroom as long as he is physically able.

At some point in time, every child will come to know a friend, teacher, or family member with AIDS. That is why AIDS education should be part of the health curriculum in every school. And because charity—and understanding—begin at home, it should be part of the ongoing communication there as well.

PHYSICALLY CHALLENGED CHILDREN

Public Law 94-142 is a federal law mandating that every public school in the United States provide a child, regardless of his handicap, with equal access to educational opportunity. This law took hundreds of thousands of physically handicapped children out of the isolation of their homes (or schools, where they were housed in separate, self-contained classrooms) and provided them with the opportunity to be mainstreamed with other children as much as possible.

This federal law, with its states' counterpart, revolutionized the way we, as a society, treat our citizens with special needs. Where once there were only curbs on sidewalks, there are now also ramps. Where once there were only stairs, there are elevators. But that doesn't mean there isn't room for improvement.

Be sure that your physically challenged child is comfortable in her educational environment. Take a walk through the school with her and note any remaining areas of difficulty. Make sure the special restrooms are equipped to serve the students and staff that need them.

Last but not least, ask the bus company whether your child can be part of the regular gang at the bus stop. Many buses are equipped to pick up wheelchairs with special lifts. Others have telephones on-board to protect the well-being of children with seizure disorders. Alterations like these can help your child feel like one of the bunch—and that can be the biggest boost of all to your challenged child's morale.

10
Public Education: A Revolution-in-Progress

If this book has convinced you of nothing else, we hope that it has shown you that our public schools *are* working, and that public school graduates go on either to college or to successful careers. But if there has been one benefit to the bad news blitz created by the media, it is this: the worst-case scenarios presented in our papers didn't just alert us to the problems now troubling our schools. They mobilized us. Now, as a direct result, more research than ever is being done in the area of educational reform. Best of all, that creative thinking is being done not just by educators and social scientists, but by the businesspeople, taxpayers, think-tank members, professionals, and parents who demanded that the school doors be opened and that they be allowed in.

As we've said, each of our public schools is a microcosm of the community that surrounds it. That's why looking at our neighborhood schools, at their strengths and deficits, is like looking into a mirror of our society. Every program that we fund, staff, or volunteer for—and every program that we don't—is a clear reflection of a community's current values. But values, like what we see in the mirror, do change with the times. In fact, they are constantly under revision. What values will our schools reflect in the year 2000? And how are the political decisions we make today likely to change the shape of education in the future?

THE SHAPE OF THINGS TO COME

Researchers and educators have invested a great deal of time and effort to look into the future of our communities and our schools. And they've come to the conclusion that there's a revolution in progress! This entire scenario for change hinges on an increasingly effective home-school partnership.

In many ways, the transition has already begun. And we were the ones who began it. The dramatic increase in two-career and single-parent families has brought the issue of federally funded childcare out of the nursery and into the forefront of the political arena. Our questions about which schools to fund and how best to fund them have made quality education every student's right—and every taxpayer's responsibility. Parental pressure for the best possible teachers brought thousands of our most gifted citizens out of the business world and into our schools. But that's only the beginning.

Considering the evidence, the trends most likely to shape the future of public education are the following:

- *Increased parental choice*. In the most recent Gallup poll of public attitudes on education, the overwhelming percentage of respondents agreed that parents should

198

have increased input into school decisions, including budgetary issues, questions of curriculum, and decisions about personnel and programs. Moreover, in the same poll, a whopping 76 percent of parents with children in public school went on to say that they should have complete freedom of choice when deciding which public school their children would attend.

Some forward-looking think-tanks have taken this concept one step farther, suggesting that public schools will perform to their potential only when a parent can choose among public *and* private schools—and invest his tax dollars in whatever school he chooses! Opinion runs the gamut on that controversial twist, but researchers agree that choice is an essential freedom whose time has come.

- *The school-based community resource center*. By 1992, two-thirds of all preschool-age children will have mothers in the work force. Many of those mothers will be single parents who are shouldering the responsibility of parenting alone. Some will be teenage mothers who need to educate themselves before they can help educate their children. Others may be caught in a dual bind: serving as nurturers to their children and as caregivers to elderly, ailing parents.

By the year 2000, your local schools will embrace and instruct all these parents, for they will have become the source of ongoing education and the focal point of community life. As you already know, schools are more conscious than ever of the whole child. To that end, many schools have adopted preschool and after-school care as a way to offer continuous learning experiences to the children they will one day educate. In the future, our schools will speak to the entire range of human experience. And they will house and deliver a vast variety of services, from school-based care to seminars for senior citizens; from parenting classes and programs for the disadvantaged to health fairs, career seminars, and support groups. In this way, our schools will be transformed from single-service facilities to centers for continuous community education.

- *Teacher development.* Right now, what we say and what we do are on a collision course. We say we want our children in small classes where they will be taught by well-trained professionals. Yet, in an effort to save tax money, we continue to offer our teachers salaries that are not competitive with other professions, limited freedom to pursue their careers, and few opportunities for professional growth. If things don't change, some analysts warn, there will be an overall teacher shortage by the year 2000.

But that shortsighted and self-defeating attitude *will* change. The startling educational study, "A Nation at Risk," opened our eyes about the shortcomings of public education—and about the ways the educational system fails our teachers. Shortly after its publication, teacher development was cited by President George Bush as one of his five goals. It was also adopted as an initiative by the NEA, the NAESP (National Association of Elementary School Principals), the NSPA (National School Psychologists Association), and many other educational associations.

By the dawn of the new century, teachers will, at last, have been accepted for the professionals they are. And as such, they will benefit from certain perks, including certification reciprocity (a regional agreement to accept another state's certification so teachers can pursue their careers wherever it is most financially rewarding); financial incentive programs to reward our most successful teachers; ongoing professional training; health fairs (with stress and cholesterol tests, to care of the caregivers); and mentor teacher programs (so our youngest teachers can learn by a mature teacher's experience).

- *More effective methods of learning.* Recent research shows that 75 percent of children learn faster and better through hands-on experiences than through passive forms of education (lecturing). Moreover, in a poll of "meritorious teachers" (conducted by the National Institute for the Improvement of Education), an overwhelming 98 percent of respondents complained that our children are not being taught decision-making skills. Not only will the schools of the future emphasize the skills students need most—like problem solving and creative thinking—they will teach those skills the way they are most efficiently learned.

  Teachers, aides, and students will all be immersed in the hands-on learning style. Throughout their training, they will learn not to offer theory but to use the materials and equipment on which a theory can be physically tested. Even parents will be trained (through the school-based community resource center) to reinforce the method at home. Teachers may even do externships, taking their skills to the sites where hands-on smarts are applied every day in business, industry, and vocational schools.

  Not only is the hands-on method more enriching, it can enhance a student's skills in diagnostics, analysis, planning, and troubleshooting.

- *An extended school year.* The school year (and even school day) will likely be extended for two reasons: our children are competing with children of other nations who attend school 240 days a year, and, with more mothers joining the work force, this will become a necessary convenience.

- *Earlier intervention.* In early 1990, the *Journal of the American Medical Association* made headlines with its groundbreaking study on the effects of early intervention on developmentally impaired, low-birthweight babies (see chapter 9). If learning activities and games designed to encourage language, social, and intellectual development can actually raise the IQ of a baby born developmentally at risk, what kind of impact could earlier intervention have on a less severely challenged youngster? It is precisely this kind of research that will ultimately spearhead the movement to intervene earlier on behalf of all kinds of challenged students—and precisely this kind of effort that may ultimately decrease our dependence on costly special education classes.

TEN IMPROVEMENTS MONEY CAN'T BUY

We can hear it right now. "Uh-oh. The educators are talking about restructuring again. Hold on to your wallets." True—the high cost of education can be a bitter pill for an overtaxed community to swallow, but maintaining the academic framework of a school can be a lot like maintaining the structure of a house. Sometimes you can get away with a patch. Other times only a complete overhaul will do.

Breaking new ground doesn't have to mean breaking the bank if you are willing to take restructuring slowly. Right now, you can improve morale, boost home-school communication, and bring your school one step closer to the twenty-first century by incorporating some of the ten low-cost, high-impact strategies outlined below. Some require a small financial outlay. Others can be accomplished with only a little volunteer time and effort. All are designed to open the school doors a little wider.

Note that these quick-fix ideas range from the esoteric to the practical—as do the needs of our schools. Because considering them will force you to get to know your schools a little better, it can be as instructive for you to consider and reject our ideas as it can be to give them a try.

- *Set up a parent information center*. At least twenty-five schools in eight states are now using "voice mail" tape systems to clue parents in daily to the subjects their kids are studying, the projects they are planning, and the dates they will be needing parent volunteers. The cost of such a computerized phone system ranges from $4,500 to $10,000 (for a school with 1,000 students).

  As an alternative that costs next to nothing, a parent information center can be established by simply setting aside a separate bulletin board at school for school-to-parent announcements. If space permits, parents can even use the board as a sign-up center where they can network for day-care providers, car pool information, or even volunteer to fulfill teachers' wish lists. Some added benefits: the in-school bulletin board bridges the gap between school as a single service facility and as a community resource center. Moreover, it brings parents physically into the schools, maximizing face-to-face contact with the principal, teachers, and staff.

- *Get free advice*. Your daughter simply refuses to do homework. Or your son has gone head-to-head with a difficult teacher—and you aren't sure what to do about it. What should you do? For the cost of a phone call, you can get personalized, professional advice through a toll-free help line set up by the National Committee for Citizens in Education. The hotline, which logs in up to 500 calls a month, puts callers in touch with educators, special ed experts, as well as parents who have been there themselves, to answer questions on any number of education-related topics. (Bilingual services are available too.)

To make the education connection, call 1-800/NET-WORK toll-free (or, in Maryland, 301/997-9300). The NCCE also offers brochures on a wide range of subjects, such as parent involvement, how to appeal school practices and policies, and how to review and request changes in your child's school records. Call for information, or write the NCCE at 10840 Little Patuxent Parkway, Suite 301, Columbia, MD 21044.

- *Establish school-age childcare.* Early morning and afterschool programs are generally considered to be high-ticket items, but they need not be. If your school principal (and school board) considers the school building a community resource, the cost of providing extended care (including paying a professional staff, increased liability insurance, heat and food costs) can ultimately be balanced by the income from this service.

  To help the childcare center become self-sufficient, require that the parents of each enrolled child volunteer as aides when needed. Ask that they provide afterschool snacks. Or ask them to organize or publicize the center. They will have the assurance of knowing that they helped engineer the center that is providing their children with care—and the school will have taken that extra step toward serving the community in a meaningful way.

- *Celebrate theme days.* Sports team appreciation day. Field day. School pride day. Career day. What a difference a day makes! Just by setting aside a few minutes or a few hours (depending on what activities are in the works) to come together as a group, your school can get a morale boost that lasts for weeks. Not only do theme days allow students to view teachers in a different—more human—light, but they give the kids a chance to shine.

Because theme days are easily tailored to suit the needs of the individual school, they are particularly effective weapons against community problems. One inner-city school recently held self-esteem day—which they marked with "why I like myself" workshops—to galvanize students against the self-deprecating world of drugs.

A theme day can even make a lesson in current events seem more like an event in itself. Students can wear the colors of the country they are studying, and perhaps, if the home cooks are feeling ambitious, sample the foods of that country. In the higher grades, teachers may set aside a week to focus on a current problem as it makes news. But even one day spent celebrating our world can help kids feel part of it all—and part of the comradery and team spirit that is the soul of a school.

- *Use the buddy system.* Set up a tutoring service between big and little kids, and you have set up one of the most natural learning enhancers in the world. Generally speaking, there is nothing a child won't do to please his older, "cooler" counterpart. And even the coolest tutor may find himself studying harder, just to earn his "reading buddy's" admiration.

- *Make education a family affair.* A child may go to school up to six hours a day, but he spends most of his waking hours with his family. Unfortunately, many

American families live in "total television households" in which the TV goes on at noon and doesn't go off until midnight.

To those families we say, set aside just one hour, twice a week, for educational enrichment, and the whole family will benefit. If money is tight, attend the story hour at your local library. Go to the zoo. Visit a museum or the historical society. Is money tighter than tight? Then go for a nature walk or on a picnic. Collect shells at the beach or cans for the recycling center. Visit the hospital nursery. Whatever you do, turn off the television long enough to get to know one another. That can be the greatest educational experience of them all.

- *Form partnerships between universities and schools.* Universities are finally beginning to understand that they are not meeting the needs of their future teachers by teaching them only theory. And teachers need to listen to the researchers who discover new educational methods and trends. By bringing these two groups together, we can educate parents, validate teachers, inspire researchers, and improve our schools.

  On the whole, collegial relationships do not occur naturally between professors and practitioners. To some university instructors, working teachers are cynical, negative, and set in their ways. They dodge recent research findings as if they were spitballs. According to many teachers, our universities simply don't train their graduates to function in real schools—or to respond to their students' real needs. We say there is nothing more practical than a good, workable idea. And if our universities will bring to us what we need most— a blueprint for successful education—then we can provide them with the framework to make their ideas real.

  It is easy to see how we would all benefit from

206

interaction between universities and local schools. The school system would be infused with brainpower. The university students could benefit from mentors teaching the hands-on experience. Professors could provide in-service work-shops and seminars to practitioners in need of ongoing education. Universities could provide a public service by researching the needs of *real*, specific schools (not "similar" schools or composites). Teaching colleges could set a good example by making involvement in the local public schools a mandatory requirement for college tenure. And to make the home-school-university link complete, these colleges could provide school-based workshops for parents as well.

- *Share your skills.* A bank can give you a return on your investment. But to make the most of a school's greatest assets (and save money to boot!), smart principals rely on the community resource bank. This is where the materials, equipment, and often the personnel come from for teaching a class through hands-on-methods.

Of all the resources that exist in the school community, parents are the greatest. As diverse and unique as their children, they bring to a school a wealth of skills and experiences that no personnel agency can match. One can teach computer. Another, a botanist, may give a lesson in why leaves change color. The owner of the local yarn shop may donate yarn and empty shipping boxes for use by the art class, while the local banker may teach the fourth grade how to balance a checkbook. (The kids may even pass along a few pointers to mom and dad.)

It takes a secure principal and teacher to invite parents to join in the day-to-day education of their children. Every time an educator or administrator opens the door to the school, she opens herself up to criticism as well as positive input. If you are in school as a resource volunteer, treat your child's teacher with all the professional respect that you would demand.

And please *do* blow your own horn when filling out any skills evaluation or resource information sheet your school may send. Educators don't mind you asking what your schools can do for you if you are willing to do something for your schools.

- *Make education a special interest.* Some special-interest groups wield a great deal of clout. It is crucial, then, that we make education a pet project of those groups.

Senior citizens have learned the merits of frugality. They simply won't vote for increased school budgets unless they can see how the money is being spent. Bring them into the schools as volunteers, aides, or instructors in their field of expertise. Business leaders can offer materials as well as the staff to do classroom demonstrations. Hospitals are a great source of speakers, health-related videotapes, and equipment and staffing for health fairs. Add to those the fire department (and at least one truck), the police (maybe the K-9 unit), and perhaps an emergency services dispatcher (to teach kids what to do in case of an emergency), and you get more opportunities for low-cost enrichment than there is time to do it all!

Your school may have a partnership-in-education coordinator whose job it is to link these groups to the needs of the school. If not, an interested group of parents, a retiree, or even a retired educator may take on the project as a volunteer.

- *Be there.* By now you have learned that grades, standardized test scores, long-term achievement rates, and student morale all go up when parents make education *their* business. Be there to check your child's homework or provide extra help, and you will stop academic problems before they start. Be there to defend your child's rights when there is a question of placement, retention, or assignment to a special classroom. Be there to encourage your child's teacher. It takes only a few kind words to smooth out the ups, downs, twists, and turns of a long, hard school year. In short, it is not enough to demand that the school doors be opened to you; you must take the initiative to walk through them.

Your school system will not become more accountable to you until you become accountable for it. Be there today to shape a plan for tomorrow. And remember: getting the best public school education for your child isn't just your right. It's your responsibility.

Recommended Readings

ALCOHOLISM

Black, Claudia. "My Dad Loves Me, My Dad Has a Disease." Mac Publishing, Denver: 1979.

Hastings, Jill, and Marion Typpo. *An Elephant in the Living Room*. Compcare, Minneapolis: 1984.

Morehouse, Ellen R., and Claire M. Scola. *Children of Alcoholics*. National Association for Children of Alcoholics, South Laguna, Cal.: 1986.

Seixas, Judith A. *Living With a Parent Who Drinks Too Much*. Green Willow Books, New York: 1979.

CHILD ABUSE

U.S. Department of Health and Human Services. *Study Findings: Study of National Incidence and Prevalence of Child Abuse and Neglect*. Washington, D.C.: Government Printing Office, 1988.

Wachter, Oralee. *No More Secrets For Me*. Little Brown, Boston: 1983.

DEATH

Buscaglia, Leo. *The Fall of Freddie the Leaf*. Charles B. Slack, Thorofare, N.J.: 1982.

Grossman, Earl A., ed. *Explaining Death to Children*. Beacon Press, Boston: 1969.

Jackson, Edgar N. *Telling a Child About Death*. Hawthorne Books, New York: 1965.

Krementz, Jill. *How It Feels When a Parent Dies*. Alfred A. Knopf, New York: 1983.

DISCIPLINE

Anderson, Luleen. *The Aggressive Child*. DHHS Publication No. (ADM) 85–71. Washington, D.C.: Government Printing Office, 1978; revised 1981; reprinted 1985.

Canter, Lee. *Assertive Discipline*. Canter Associates, Cal.: 1976.

DIVORCE

Grollman, Earl A. *Talking About Divorce and Separation*. Beacon Press, Boston: 1975.

Krementz, Jill. *How It Feels When Parents Divorce*. Alfred A. Knopf, New York: 1988.

Sinberg, Janet. *Divorce is a Grown Up Problem*. Avon Publishers, New York: 1978.

Stein, S. B. *An Open Family Book for Parents and Children Together*. Walker, New York: 1979.

GIFTED CHILDREN

David, G. A. *Creativity Is Forever*. Badger Press, Cross Plains, Wisconsin: 1981.

The Gifted Child Today. G.C.Y. Publishing, Mobile, Alabama.

HYPERACTIVE CHILDREN

Coleman, Wendy. *Attention Deficit Disorders, Hyperactivity and Associated Disorders*, 5th ed. Calliope, Madison, Wis.: 1988.

Wender, Paul H. *The Hyperactive Child, Adolescent and Adult*. Oxford University Press, New York: 1987.

ILLNESS

Alyson, Sasha, ed. *You Can Do Something About AIDS*. Public service project of the publishing industry, 1988.

LATCHKEY CHILDREN

Long, Lynette, and Thomas Long. *The Handbook for Latchkey Children and Their Parents*. Arbor House, New York: 1983.

LEARNING STYLES

Johnson, David, and Roger T. Johnson. *Learning Together and Alone: Cooperation, Competition, and Individualization*. Prentice Hall, Englewood Cliffs, N.J.: 1975.

U.S. Department of Education. *What Works: Research About Teaching and Learning*, 2d ed. Government Printing Office, Washington, D.C.: 1987.

MAKING FRIENDS

Ferretti, Fred. *The Great American Book of Sidewalk, Stoop, Dirt, Curb, and Alley Games*. Workman, New York: 1975.

Gurian, A., and R. Formanek. *The Socially Competent Child*. Houghton Mifflin, Boston: 1983.

Oppenheim, J., B. Boegehold, and B. Benner. *Raising a Confident Child*. Pantheon, New York: 1984.

Steiner, Claude. *The Original Warm Fuzzy Tail*. Jalmar Press, Sacramento, Cal.: 1983.

Wilt, J. *A Kid's Guide to Making Friends*. Word, 1978.

MULTICULTURAL EDUCATION

Gollnick, Donna M., and Phillip C. Chinn. *Multicultural Education in a Pluralistic Society*. Charles E. Merrill, New York: 1986.

SINGLE PARENTS

Gardner, Richard A. *The Boys and Girls Book About One Parent Families*. Bantam Books, New York: 1983.

SPECIAL NEEDS

Meyer, D. J., P. F. Vadasy, and R. R. Felwell. *Living with a Brother or Sister with Special Needs*. University of Washington Press, Seattle: 1985.

STEPFAMILIES

Gardner, R. *The Boys and Girls Book About Stepfamilies*. Gardner, Palo Alto, Cal.: 1982.

Stenson, Janet Sinberg. *Now I Have a Stepparent and It's Kind of Confusing*. Avon Books, New York: 1979.

STRESS

Arent, R. P. *Stress and Your Child*. Prentice Hall, Englewood Cliffs, N.J.: 1984.

Kersey, K. *Helping Your Child Handle Stress*. Acropolis, Washington, D.C.: 1985.

Medeiros, Donald C., Barbara J. Porter, and I. David Welch. *Children Under Stress*. Prentice Hall, Englewood Cliffs, N.J.: 1983.

Herskowitz, Joel. *Is Your Child Depressed?* Pharos Books, New York: 1988.

SUICIDE

Hicks, Barbara Barrett. *Youth Suicide, A Comprehensive Manual for Prevention and Intervention*. National Educational Service, Bloomington, Indiana: 1990.

Index

217